AROS

where barbarians are truly barbaric
where warriors are not always noble
where heroines are not necessarily virgins
and where heroes are rarely indefatigable

AROS

where the world as we know it does not
exist but does in fact abide . . .

ARDOR
ON AROS

an outrageously inventive novel
of crossed swords and sorceries,
careening adventures and sublime
paradoxes.

ARDOR ON AROS

Andrew J. Offutt

A DELL BOOK

to
Helen S. Offutt
who Knew
when no one else
even cared

Published by
Dell Publishing Co., Inc.
1 Dag Hammarskjold Plaza
New York, New York 10017
Copyright © 1973 by Andrew J. Offutt
Dell ® TM 681510, Dell Publishing Co., Inc.
Printed in the United States of America
First printing—May 1973

PROLOGUE

While it is true that I have written some mildly imaginative stories, I am a businessman. I think my readers will corroborate that I have written nothing like the narrative that follows. This one was dictated to me— or rather into my office tape recorder—on five consecutive nights. I cannot tell you how, although on the day of the first transmission I had mentioned the narrator while dictating a letter on that same recorder. I recognize the name, if not his voice. (I admit mine is not the best of recorders.)

The file folder is one of only two with the helpless notation: LAPSED. WHEREABOUTS UNKNOWN.

Whereabouts unknown! None of my other clients, however far-flung, has ever traveled so far. But I will let him tell his own story, through this transcription of the tapes. I am only the mouthpiece for my former client and his strange story.* I have not even corrected some of the narrator's errors. There is a certain charm in the narration, from the mind and lips of one who has no reference books at hand and does not pretend to have all the answers.

*At the request of the narrator, I have turned over the cassette tapes themselves to the library of Morehead State University. The tapes are available there for listening, on request. Or you may write to Box P, Morehead, Kentucky. Hopefully the royalties from this narrative will enable the college officials to reply.

I can assure you it is unlike any adventure you have ever read, although it is astonishingly similar to some, as if it were the prototype. But here you will find no omniscient, indefatigable, undefeatable superhero. The barbarians *are* barbarians; real men with drives, emotions, and genitalia. They are not painted, as they have been by other mouthpieces, bigger than life. They will appeal to those of us Conan Doyle referred to when he wrote

> I have wrought my simple plan
>   If I give one hour of joy
> To the boy who's half a man,
>   Or the man who's half a boy.

andrew j. offutt
Funny Farm
Morehead, Kentucky   40351
March 1972

CONTENTS

1.
The scientist
who was not mad

Mine was one of those wasted college careers: before miniskirts, marijuana, and muggings. All I got from four years in an American college—a place where we went not to learn but to obtain a lanolinized union card guaranteeing a job—was a fair but mostly useless education and a basic grounding in human psychology: from the classroom, from a few of the many required books written by the professors and their old school chums, and mostly from participation in campus politics, and the best source, other human beings.

Let's get the unfortunate part said fast: I've never had any physics, and the only hard science courses I took were General Science 101-102. Standard Freshman Requirements. I never took fencing either.

I was a fair shot and a fast thinker with good reflexes before I got to college. Yoga I studied on my own, without ever mastering it. I really don't like being pushed, and disliked the useless ant colony of college "education."

I am—was—a sort of Southerner, by the way. My state, to its shame, supplied the leader to each side in the war that gave Mississippi highway patrolmen the traitors' flag they brandish in their front license plate holders.

I start with college because I'm not interested in making a Stendahlian Great Confession of my childhood. It wasn't all that hungup, anyhow, and normal childhoods aren't the thing to write about.

When I left school I hadn't the foggiest notion who I was, what I was doing, or where I was going. Where I was at, in the then current terminology that destructed years of grade-school training. Is the expression still in use, on Earth? Lord, I remember one teacher who stood us in a corner for two hours if we ended a sentence with "to" or "at." Same old girl who wouldn't allow us to use nicknames. Called everyone by his birth certificate name, no matter what even his parents preferred. I hated my name then, particularly the formal version: Henry. Ukh. I wanted to be called Rocky. I hated that old bag, too. She's in her grave now, along with most of what she represented: changelessness and the old Victorian formality and morality.

It hasn't come back, has it?

Like a lot of students, I wasn't ready to be a graduate, an adult.

It happens pretty fast, that graduation-and-turning-loose. Yesterday you were subject to the dean and dorm rules; today you're supposed to be a man. I'd no idea what I wanted to do. Get married? Like a lot of males my age I was a lot more enchanted with the concept of living in sin. I even considered the Peace Corps. It seemed a good enough place for someone trying to find some answers (The Answer!), and most of us students were pretty much wide-eyed idealists in those days. Dad had made money, and Things. Since we had 'em we could afford to sneer at them and concentrate on changing the world. (To what? We didn't know. Did Jefferson and Franklin, or Gaius Julius Caesar?)

I wanted to be a Nobel winner, another Sigmund Freud or Oliver Cromwell—in reverse: I considered going about taking an ax to Fundamentalist churches. I wanted to be a writer. I knew what I didn't want to do: I didn't want to fly a Huey in Vietnam. I didn't want a uniform: Modern Army Green or Navy Blue or Air Force Blue or Madison Avenue gray, either. Maybe I wanted to climb the Matterhorn, explore the sea bottom, be an astronaut, get involved in human cloning, bomb the Vatican to try to Do Something about the population mess. Maybe hunt: tigers in India or for a lost explorer in Africa. (But none get lost anymore: Hemingway and his better, Ruark, left trails of gin bottles to follow.)

Instead I snapped up an intriguing Opportunity: sort of secretary, sort of assistant, to Dr. Finley Blakey. He knew I didn't know where I was going, knew I was pretty bright, and he liked me. So I took the job —at $450 a month. But I didn't need money and I didn't worry about that end of it. I figured any man should spend a few years profiting by experience; in his head, rather than in his pocket. I had plenty of time for the great American pastime, the run for the money. Besides, that's about what the high priest of management consultants, Peter Drucker, was saying —and Dr. Blakey had enough pull to get me a deferment.

Finley Blakey had two Masters' degrees and an Sc.D. in addition to his Ph.D. He also had myopia, two cats, a dog, a verminously scummy parrot, bad breath, and one of the most brilliant minds on the hemisphere. He was one of those old-time oddballs: hated Feds and rules and sweated it out with a home laboratory, which the Feds were certain could not be done, to any purpose. One had to have staffs, committee decisions, $9000-a-year secretaries and all that. Dr. Blakey wasn't interested in all that: security, a badge (belongingness and status), several assistants and secretaries, a regular salary, and that hospitalization plan you can't buy but that even your mongoloid postal clerk has. (Have they made it a private corporation yet?)

Dr. Blakey WAS absent-minded; that's a normal adjunct of genius. He was a scientist. He was NOT mad.

Kooky, yes. Mad, no.

He was working on Something Big. I didn't know what. I spent most of my time trying to discover what he and his assistant were doing. Now I know: that's what they were doing, too! His assistant was going to write her doctoral thesis around their work, and I suppose she's long since published and earned that ultimate union card. But I'll bet her conclusion's wrong. Things sure can't be depended upon to be as they seem!

I did what I was told, trying to soak up what I could while observing the genius at work. *If he succeeds at whatever-it-is,* I thought, *I'll be famous.* (I probably was, too, for a few days—was I?) His wife and the dog and his assistant did essentially what I did, while the cats and the parrot did what they pleased. The parrot was named Pope Borgia.

I never did learn where Dr. Blakey got his backing. I wrote letters to somebody named Gordon, mostly demanding more equipment or the money to buy it. Mr. Gordon called every now and then. I didn't eavesdrop. There wasn't an extension phone.

I admit I was more interested than anything else in the bulges in his assistant's lab smock, fore and aft. Evelyn unfortunately was more interested in her work than in me. Which led to painful discussions:

"I think you must be a satyr," she told me, pronouncing it: "say-tah." "You must be. You really don't think of anything else, do you?"

I went along. "Nope. I belong to a disadvantaged

minority group called males. God laid on us a mandate: *fill women.* But cool it on the Freudian inreading. Satyriasis is a serious illness. Permanently up."

"And with you it's only ninety percent of the time."

"Evelyn, we are a young man and a young woman thrown together by circumstances. It is kismet. It is only natural, only fitting, that we—"

"You're an adventurer," she said. ("You ah an adventuah.") Evelyn, blonde hair and bulges or not, was a scientist, and worse, an American. Neither can stand to see things go unlabeled. Sure she was a bright young physicist. But I still call her Intellectually Disadvantaged. She probably got her jollies from a slide rule. Looking at it, I mean.

"I'll accept that," I said, in the teeth of her baleful look. "I'd *like* to be an adventurer. A knight in armor, rescuing white-smocked damsels from wizards in evil laboratories." I eyed her knees. In the fashions of the time, the only way a woman could avoid having her knees eyed was to wear a bathrobe or pants —in which case she got her fanny eyed. What are they wearing now, those nonsorcerous women of Earth?

She got up off Dr. Blakey's couch. "Hank, you ah ridiculous. Go—wait, one question: what are you going to do when you grow up?"

"Oh boy. That's supposed to tear me up," I said, torn up. "Be a fireman?"

She waited.

"Be a writer," I sighed. "What about you?"

But her blue eyes had widened. "Really? Seriously?" She sounded breathless, and I hastened to assure her I would be the Great American writer. She sat back down. I soon found out why: she was writing a novel. Naturally she wanted an audience; every

would-be writer does. Maybe I was good for something after all.

Angling for barter, I asked her what she and Dr.
Blakey had been doing in the lab today.

There'd been a flap that afternoon: Something Happened in the lab. Cries. Exclamations. Much rushing
about and shouting, followed by muttering and a
phone call to Gordon and secret dictation. But Dr.
Blakey must've mailed the tape itself. When I sat down
to type, practically falling all over myself in my eager-
ness, all that little plug said in my ear was blah
correspondence and such blah notes. There *was* a
reference to "the experiment." I typed it in caps: The
Experiment. Dr. Blakey didn't complain.

But Evelyn wouldn't tell me. So I stupidly advised her to take her blank-blank story as a supposi-
tory, and I stalked off. (Paper tigers, yeah I know.
But the two of them were destroying my male ego.)

It happened again next day, whatever it was, again
behind closed and locked (I checked) laboratory
doors. Shouts. Exclamations. Pitter-patter-*pat*. Delighted outcries. Odd noises. Telephone to Gordon.
Secret dictation. I even tried the lab door at one A.M.
Locked. And guarded—damn that bigmouthed parrot!

In the morning Dr. Blakey interrupted my work.

"Hank, I want to make you a proposition."

"Dr. Blakey!"

"Oh dear god, Henry, let's don't play freshman
games. [Ouch! No paper tiger, him!] I want to in-
volve you in my work—but first I want you to swear
yourself to secrecy, and I mean from *anyone*. Anyone."

I fixed his eyes, huge behind his superspecs, with
my own, so far back in my head they're barely visi-
ble. "Done," I said.

He hesitated. "That was very fast," he observed. "But—somehow I believe you mean it."

"Dr. Blakey, you yourself told me it's getting harder and harder to find someone who makes fast decisions. I do. A couple of odd but positive things have happened in the lab this week, and you want another head and a pair of eyes involved, even unscientific mine. But it's secret, and I'm curious. I'll swap absolute silence for a look at what you've been afraid to let me type about."

He regarded me thoughtfully. His eyes neither narrowed nor widened nor blinked. Nor did his mouth drop open, or any of that TV business. He merely gazed at me.

"Amazing," he said at last, in a perfectly normal tone. "Your father's totally wrong about you! I suppose you know he thinks you are a—, a—"

"—wastrel; stupid ass; et cetera," I supplied. "But yes, I have a brain. It works, fairly often. I enjoy using it. Also—I'm a nonscience type. We're number two these days. We try harder."

He smiled; he's fond of TV, and knows every commercial. Jingles are all he whistles—badly. "Come along, Hank."

I went along. Into the lab.

There's no sense describing it, is there? You've seen movies and TV. You see one home-grown lab, you've seen 'em all. All this one lacked was Igor and a Jacob's ladder. Oh—and Vincent Price. Dr. Blakey looked more like Roger Price. And Evelyn looked more like the Mad Scientist's blonde captive than his co-worker.

"Hank, keep your eyes on that platform and the glass bell and the contents at all times. Do not take your eyes from it. Please note all times exactly. Here, use this." He handed me his cassette recorder and

microphone. I nodded without pointing out that I'd
have to take my eyes off the bell and platform to
check my watch. That would have been more "freshman games," no doubt. I'd noticed he seemed to have
lost his pocket watch.

The little platform and the big glass bell didn't look
partcularly impressive. The platform was metal—
meteoric, as it turned out, a sort of Blakeyesque
home-brew from something that plopped down in his
daddy's backyard when he was eleven. Dr. B, not his
father. The platform was precisely, I learned later,
four feet by four feet. The bell covered it exactly and
was four feet tall—precisely.

Dr. Blakey and Evelyn—looking very labbish in a
long white coat, although the dirty seat in back and
thrust in front detracted somewhat—exchanged
meaningful looks. I so advised the microphone,
quietly.

"Dr. Blakey is now approaching the platform. Now
he is taking his ball-point pen from the breast pocket
of his lab coat. It is 11:17. It is a gold pen, made by
Cross, given him for Christmas by Mr. Gordon about
whom I'm supposed to know nothing. I put a new
cartridge into it yesterday: blue. It has a lifetime
guarantee. He is placing it on the platform at . . . exactly 11:18 Ay Em. He turns to look at Miss Shay and
he nods. At me. I nod. He steps back. The gold ball-
point looks very tiny, there on the platform. Now he
has depressed a button; the glass bell is descending
to—11:19—cover the platform. It makes a clanging
sound. Dr. Blakey says the air is being drawn from
the airtight chamber thus formed. Again he looks at
us. We both nod. He returns to the platform, peers into it, at the pen—it is 11:20 and a half. I believe his
glasses need changing; make a note to remind
him. Again he looks signif—11:21—icantly at both of

us. I nod. Evel—Miss Shay—waits, looking very anxious. Waiting. 11:22. I can see the pen. Is something
supposed to happen to it? Dr. Blakey is looking at the
pen. Ev—Miss Shay—is looking at Dr. Blakey. It is—
11:25. Dr. Blakey nods and snaps his fingers without
looking up—tells me to watch the pen—it is 11:26—
Miss Shay closes a relay—the pen IS GONE!"

We looked at each other.

Dr. Blakey pushed his finger into his ear and wiggled it.

"Very good, Hank. You recorded every step and
kept excellent track of time. Do by all means remind
me about my spectacles—better still, call Dr. what's-
'is-name for an appointment. Make three, as soon as
possible; I'll try to keep one of them. Well, Miss
Shay."

Miss Shay—and Hank. Relative importance, of
course.

"Oh—yes. Well. That's three times, doctor."

We were sitting in what Dr. Blakey calls his study
—it was meant to be a dining room. It was 2 P.M., we
had not had lunch, we had just listened to my tape,
we were having, at Dr. Blakey's suggestion, a very
large brandy-soda. I swigged mine with the usual
covered-up shudder.

"Please tell me."

Dr. Blakey looked at me. "Henry, at 11:25—and
probably a half—this morning, my gold Cross pen vanished. At 3:15 yesterday my chiming watch also vanished. From the same platform, in the same manner,
apparently instantaneously as the relay was closed."

I sighed and pulled at the brandy soda (heavy on
Coronet; light on IGA soda). I remember thinking
that Dr. Blakey was playing hell keeping gold in the
country.

"Yes sir. But sir—where? I mean—vanished to *where?*"

"Henry, in a word—we do not know." He favored my gaping mouth with a benign smile. "I call that platform and the materials, that, uh, motivate it, a temporal dissociator."

"Sir?"

"Time machine," Evelyn Shay said.

"Time machine," Dr. Blakey said, not without some sign of irritation. " 'Time machine,' however, is a fictional phrase, an over-used one, and it has been proved impossible. I could not even discuss it with the editor of my favorite magazine, *Engineering Analogies,* for he considers time, uh, travel to be fantasy, and his mind is closed until and unless I allow some university dean to drive it to his office, with blueprints. But—I cannot *prove* that it is a 'time machine,' of course." (His eyebrows placed the quote-marks around the phrase.) "Nevertheless, two solid objects have been placed on the platform and both have vanished. Unfortunately we know neither to where, nor to *when,* if we may invent a new phrase." He looked thoughtful. "And I think perhaps we must." He rose to his feet, swirling the amber liquid in his glass. It was a peanut-butter glass.

"I propose we try to think of something else. I must make notes—Henry, you will type these, and I remind you of your secrecy pledge. Tomorrow—tomorrow we shall experiment once again, this time with a live subject: Pope Borgia."

Poor ole Pope, I thought, secretly delighted. Loudmouthed bighead!

Doctor Blakey departed. Evelyn and I stared at each other.

"Marry me," I said, "and let me take you away from all this."

"Oh god, Hank, shut up!"

"OK. Where, O Iron Maiden dedicated to Science, did Dr. Blakey's hardware go?"

She spread her hands. "Even *he* doesn't know. The future? ("Fū chah." Sounds pretty.) The past? 10 B.C.? The Pleistocene? Maybe tomorrow; maybe tomorrow he'll have his pen back again. Maybe key, pen, and paper are in the LaBrea Tar Pits. Or Waukegan. We're trying to find out, Hank."

"In other words, male secretary, don't bug us geniuses."

She looked contrite. "Oh Hank—"

I had her contrite, which was enough for starts, and I pursued by swinging off on another track. "Oh god, Evelyn," I sighed, "give me your manuscript." I needed to think of something else. Too, I thought, the flattery of being asked for her story should aid my amorous angling.

Her eyes were suddenly bright, her voice unscientifically eager. That manuscript was her go-button, all right! I hoped it would lead me to her other one. "Let me read it to you."

If she'd had a tail she'd have wagged it. Interesting idea; *let's keep Pope Borgia,* I thought, *and send Iron Evelyn. And her cute li'l tail.*

I watched it switch as she went for her manuscript. I typed up the notes. Including this description of the temporal dissociator, which didn't tell me much:

"When brass plates A & B (cf. enclosed diagram) are opposite each other, the two fixed plates A & C may be considered as one mass, in accord with Kohlrausch's law. Anode plate B, together with diode plate D, constitute another mass. These masses do *not* possess the same electric state. Using an electrowinning, nonaqueous solution plus the harnessed—and long recognized—electrical current emitted by *my own brain waves,* I have succeeded in forcing the two masses AC-DB into separate spatiotemporal existences. As the bell descends, a proportional augmentation of this peculiar property is achieved, reaching its maximum when the contacts on the bell are firmly joined with the brass plates on the platform itself. A strong electromotive force is instantaneously impressed across all terminals. *Within the bell, 'reality' as we know it does not exist.* Any foreign object (sendee) contained there perforce vanishes—with no manifestation of the resultant phenomenon we call 'breaking the sound barrier'; that is, no vacuum pocket is created by the departure of the foreign body.

"Thus the object introduced into the mechanism, the *sendee, cannot* have ceased to exist, or to have been transported to another area in space as we know it. Rejecting outright fantasy then, my thesis is that the *sendee* is transferred through time. A simple perusal of Professor Einstein's quaint concept of 'time' will indicate clearly why this must, empirically, be so."

There you are. You're welcome.

"My name," Evelyn began, "is Achilles Caxton."
"You're a *man?*"
She looked up accusingly. I looked down. "You're a man," I said. "Sorry. It was a surprise. After all, how many novels have surprise *beginnings?*"

Which brought something approaching a simper, and she continued to read. "I was born in Virginia, rather well-born, as a matter of fact. I was well-educated, graduating from Harvard as captain of the football and fencing teams and salutatorian with a prelaw degree in political science and history."

I refrained from groaning. Achilles Caxton sounded like Frank Merriwell. Just a bit much.

"Since I had by my education increased my value to my country," Evelyn continued reading, not noticing my masked reaction, "it immediately made use of my intellect and education. My services began in Fort Benning, Georgia, and four months later I was in the mystic Orient. Three days after my arrival in Vietnam, I was driving the Colonel's jeep, the army having in its inscrutable wisdom decided this was the duty for which I was best suited, to the Officers' Club in Saigon. It was one of those clear nights when the stars and planets are bright, twinkling gems in an indigo sky, and the cry of the numerous Saigon *filles de joie* wafted loud and clear through the city."

I laughed; Evelyn beamed. *Hey,* I thought, *she doesn't sound so prudish, on paper. She's an interesting mixture. Dream-fantasist?*

"I was rankling, I admit, at my duties; as I waited impatiently, engine idling, for the passage of an oxcart, I gazed up at a ruddy spot in the sky. A child's marble, it appeared, tossed carelessly there and named for the war-god of Rome. Mars. How I'd love to be there! Anywhere but here. Anywhere but—

"The tarpaulin on the back of the oxcart suddenly flipped back. A child, a long-haired girl of no more than twelve, bobbed up. Grinning at me, she tossed something. I ducked instinctively. The dark, fist-sized missile whished past my head. In the back seat, the Colonel strove to catch it, bobbled, and the grenade fell to the floor of our jeep and blew up. My last thought was that I'd never live to see Mars!

"I am sure we were both killed instantly, but when I awoke, I saw that there were two moons in the strangely clear sky.

"I was on Mars!"

I interrupted. "Uh—Evelyn—it sounds mighty familiar. That pretty much repeats the openings of at least two famous novels by the author of about eighty books."

Evelyn grinned in delight, ignoring my callously cast aspersions. "You recognize it? Mahvelous! You know Burroughs?"

Sure, I knew Burroughs, and since it's rather integral to my own weird story, let's explore the writing of Edgar Rice Burroughs for a moment. (I will give you Evelyn's and my discussion later.)

His first novel, A PRINCESS OF MARS, was published as a magazine serial in 1912. Pursued by a band of Indians, Captain John Carter of Virginia takes refuge in a cave, where he falls asleep thinking of the Red Planet. He awakes on Mars! Then begins a series of adventures, mainly concerned with very bad men, monsters both good and bad, sexless damsels in distress, and some fascinating customs. Mars is dying; its people have forgotten most of the great science they possessed before the cataclysmic days when their seas dried up. Their only land conveyance is a colorful eight-legged *thoat*. They also have "fliers," open aircraft rather like great rafts that move very swiftly through the thin Martian air. They possess deadly radium pistols and, like the men of the American old West, they never go out without 'em. But they also carry dagger and sword (two). These are their main fighting weapons—they fight a lot, but using the radium guns isn't cricket. Generally speaking, only villains use them in dire exigency; the good guys always fence. Like John Carter.

Carter is more agile than anyone else on Mars (there are thousands of people, red, yellow, green, and *true* white, not your Earthly pink-tan), since he is lighter (lower gravity, remember?). He is also, as he constantly reminds his reader, the finest swordsman on two planets. He does a great deal of killing, a great deal of getting captured, and a great deal of rescuing—mostly women. Chastely. Mostly one woman: his Dejah Thoris (by his own constant admission the most beautiful woman on two planets). She is the daughter of the ruler of Mars's greatest city, and so John Carter gets to be crown prince: "warlord." John Carter apparently possesses no genitalia, nor does Dejah.

In another of Burroughs' Mars books, Ulysses Paxton is killed—sort of. He wakes up on Mars, whole, where he has a lot of adventures and marries a princess. Chastely. So does Carson Napier, another Edgar Rice Burroughs (ERB) hero, who crash-lands on Venus. It's just as barbaric and weird as ERB's Mars: monsters, triple-dyed villains, flying men, strange races, rayguns and swords, lots of capturing and rescuing and escaping. Carson marries a princess, and they live adventurously but chastely ever after.

Many of the further adventures of the ERB heroes were set into motion by their various womenfolk —Dejah Thoris of Mars, Duare of Venus, Dian the Beautiful of Pellucidar, Jane of Greystoke Manor, etc. Constantly borne off by a succession of black-hearted, double-dyed villains. Despite fantastic periods of separation, each Burroughs hero remained ever constant to his one true love. Nor were the kidnaped beauties raped.

The people of ERB-places are utter barbarians. Life is cheap; extremely cheap. Blood flows like words from a politico's mouth. But, while the rulers are pretty much Jenghiz Khan, there is great *honour*, and all the good guys live strictly by the code—unless you count Carter's constant goading of others into fighting him. But usually: swords, no guns. No back-stabbing. And most incredible of all: these barbarians treat women by Arthurian Table-Round rules. Very chivalrous. Courtly manners. Lots of capturing and kidnaping (with intent either to punish the husband or marry the girl). But nary a rape. Just the sort of thing for Evelyn to write.

Well, I'm a Burroughs fan, whatever his shortcomings, but—. The status of women in a barbaric culture is almost invariably lower than a snake's rectum. They're tolerated, as chattel. They are gifts: servants, cooks, bedmates, and child-rearers, to bring up more sons to murder and rape and die gloriously. Rape's as common as peanuts at a ballgame. You either kill 'em or rape 'em. Why kidnap a girl and not use her, unless she's as homely as Aunt Stella, with a body like Twiggy's or your local DAR president?

I said as much to Evelyn Shay, bright young physicist and aspiring author.

"But . . . but . . . respect for women, Hank. I mean—"

"Respect for women my eye! Oh look, Evelyn, I've always loved Burroughs, paradoxical aspect or not —*and* Otis Kline, *and* Ralph Farley."

I did. Certainly I never thought then I'd have the personal opportunity—very personal—to prove or disprove that one most jarring note. Did these barbarians really differ from every barbarian society of Earth, or was ERB merely reflecting the Victorian morality of his times toward what he called "base animal passions"?

Despairing of getting into her lab smock, I at last told Evelyn to go write me the next chapter. I ate, and I wondered where those little items of Dr. Blakey's went, and I fumed, and I went outside. I walked, and I looked at the sky. It was clear, and Mars was very clear, a red-rimmed hole in the black curtain, twinkling. I stared at it, thought about it, prompted by Evelyn's typescript and our talk.

Nothing happened, of course. There ain't no life on Mars. But how my romantic mind longed to be a part of the savage but chivalrous world of John Carter! Where white was white, and villains black, and solutions simple: instant scabbard justice. *(You can't fence,* I reminded myself.) I went in to bed.

And no, this *isn't* going to be one of those stories.

At two minutes to noon next day we sent poor Pope Borgia—raising hell all the while—off to parts or times unknown. Not a sign remained, not even a scrawk or a green feather. At 2:00 Dr. Blakey left for his meeting with Gordon. Evelyn and I talked about Pope Borgia and about her novel. She'd been thinking, she said, and I was right: she was changing the novel. Barbaric as Jenghiz Khan's Mongols, the men would treat their women the same way. I thought I saw something flicker in her eyes, and I made my pass. It was 4:13. Evelyn repulsed me.

"You want to be ravished by force, me proud beauty," I grinned, grabbing—and she showed me a judo throw. My flying elbow accidentally closed the relay. The bell began to descend—with me under it. At something like 4:16 or :17 I started to get up, stumbled, and fell. My head barely missed gonging the descending bell. I was just able to jerk in my legs —and the bell thumped down.

I didn't even have time to yell. The air whished out and my head roared and I saw red and then black and felt blood rushing from my nostrils. Then—blotto. Sorry; time unknown.

2.
The planet
that was not Mars

I lay there with my eyes closed, unable to understand what had happened, what was happening. I
must have died! But—I vaguely remembered a moment of pain, *after* the blackout, a tearing, a blurring
of everything, and a great rushing sensation. And
blankness, and—now.

I opened my eyes. I was not staring at the bell, or
at the lab ceiling.

I was staring at the sky.

Let me amend that; I was staring at *a* sky. It
was not a sky I had ever seen before, or hoped to. It
was very bright, the clouds extraordinarily pronounced
in their wispy, orange-tinted shapes, floating on a yellow sky. Yellow! A very pale orange, really; fulvous.
The sun was an enormous orange ball hanging high in
a sky it tinged ruddy with its brightness, its nearness.

Slowly, I sat up. It didn't take me four seconds
to realize something else of considerable significance:
I was naked.

I got to my feet, feeling a little vertiginous, but not
what I'd call weak. As a matter of fact, I felt fresh,
light, as if I'd just had a long rest and was in superb
condition.

I was on some sort of yellowish dust plain, stretching as far as I could see, darkening as it merged into
a sky of nearly the same hue. It was not eye-dazzling,
box-top yellow, but a pale one, more like an artist's
well-toned pastels. Slowly, I turned. Here and there

the jejune plain was dotted with boulders and rock outcrops of various sizes, as if some long-ago giant had dropped them casually, *en passant*. And then I turned completely, and I saw that I was at the base of a mountain, rising at an ever-increasing angle to brush the sky. It was orange, and yellow, and red, and there was some russet, and brown, and an occasional patch of green.

Where was I? How had I come here, at the base of this mountain, towering above this perdurable plain of yellow dust?

The answer was simple: the gizmo Dr. Blakey called a "Temporal Dissociator"—wasn't. It was a Spatial Dissociator, if anything. I wasn't on Earth!

I looked down. Yes, it was still me, and I was still naked. But there was a difference; I seemed somehow more trim. I exclaimed aloud—and froze. My voice was loud in the stillness. Wherever I was, there were no birds, no insects, no little animals, no engine sounds. And neither smoke nor smog.

I was very alone.

Also curious, and elated, and again I bent my head to peer down at myself. Suddenly I wasn't sure it was me, or, more properly put, that I was I. Here was something I'd missed when I had examined myself a minute ago, sitting down.

I've never had much stomach. I've always stayed in condition, and exercised, and haven't had to worry much about what I eat. Still, I'm human, and a product of civilization, of the American Carbohydrate Civilization, and there was a *little* soft swell to my gut.

Not any more. I was as flat below the midriff as a New York model—lying on her back.

I kept frowning, examining. But yes, this was my

old scar—about as big as a minute—on my finger, where I'd raised a blister with a cigaret and let the thing heal without trimming the dead skin off; it healed crookedly, with a little lump of skin. How many people have one of those, on the inside of the right ring finger?

I stared, bug-eyed. *I* didn't. I had a scar on the inside of my *left* ring finger, and I'd kidded and been kidded about whether there'd be trouble when some girl tried to put a wedding ring on me. My scar had moved from my left hand to my right!

I raised my right hand. That is, my brain said: *Right hand, rise.*

But my *left* hand rose. I gazed at it. *Raise left leg,* I ordered. Up came my right leg.

It was easy to check out, of course. All I had to do was feel my heart. Simple—no clothes. But it took me several seconds; my heart is now under my right pectoral. I wondered whether I were really here; I was obviously a mirror image. I had no explanation. I couldn't even explain where I was, or how. But I'm here, and have been for years, and I'm still reversed. So's my watch, but I haven't got to that yet. And remember I did tell you: things are not as they seem. How can you be sure you exist? There is no objective way.

"Where am I? What place is this, where I'm built like something Praxiteles sculpted?" I smiled as I shouted the words, and, in a sudden asinine burst of elation, I let out a yell and sprang into the air.

Way into the air. I soared up a good six feet, coming down rather slowly, as if in a dream, ten feet away from where I'd been. I sank nearly to my knees to absorb the shock of my landing, but there was really little shock to begin with. Not the shock that should have accompanied alighting after such an Olympic standing jump!

"My god! Last night I was thinking about Mars— just like Burroughs' John Carter and Paxton. I woke somewhere else—just as they did. And I'm light—just as they were. Because this isn't Earth. There's less air pressure on this world, less gravity! I *am* lighter! That's why I have such a flat gut—it's lighter here, and my innards are sort of floating up, instead of being dragged down by Earth's gravity! If I were older and had chins—they'd be gone too. This . . . this is . . . I must be on Barsoom, ERB's Mars!"

For fun, I did it again, this time *trying*. I went up a good eight feet and sailed (I paced it off, returning to my tracks), fourteen feet. A cloud of yellow dust flew up when I landed. The stuff lay everywhere, generally to a wind-swirled depth of about an inch, although there were some smallish mounds here and there, against rocks. Its density was obviously, uh, designed for this planet. Thus it settled even more quickly than I'd have expected on Earth. I sneezed, three times, and got the heck away from it.

Then I looked up at the sun, and I frowned again.

No, this isn't Mars. And it isn't Venus, or Mercury, or anything else in our solar system. Because "solar system" means "sun system," and that isn't *my* sun up there in the yellow-orange sky! It's a younger sun (or older; I can't remember if a sun cools *to* orange or builds slowly up through orange, red, yellow, white-hot—and where does blue-white come in? Sorry I can't be more precise, but you have the references to check. I haven't, and I've read a lot of books but never wasted my time memorizing things I can—could, on Earth—look up). It's also a lot closer, or a lot bigger than the sun of Earth.

Naked, I was toasty warm standing on that plain at the base of a brightly colored mountain. If I found anything here resembling people, I was sure they'd wear either next to nothing or perhaps the coolth-trapping, heat-reflecting robes worn in the Arab countries on Earth.

Leather harnesses, like Carter? Swords and zap guns?

Anyhow, I had been unaccountably transported to another planet—under another sun! I wasn't just thousands or millions of miles from Earth (I *thought*); I was several light-years, and that is a hell of a long way!

Light-years from Earth. Judging by what I could see from where I stood, I was on an uninhabited planet under a young sun—as it grew hotter, would it destroy this world and the life on it—if there was any? (Not I; I'd be long since dead.) Dead—alone.

I admit it freely. I was scared.

I stood there naked under an orange sun and started shivering like a teenager on his first date. Sweat poured off me to make pockmarks, tiny craters, in the yellow dust.

Then I heard the voice.

"Help!" it said, and it sounded weak and faraway. "Help. . . ."

I stopped breathing to listen. Again I turned all about, straining to hear. A voice! A human voice.

"I'm here!" I yelled. "Keep calling! Keep calling! I'll follow the sound of your voice!"

" h e l p. . . ." Very weak.

Yes—it definitely emanated from behind me, and I turned to face: the mountain! Perhaps that explained why I had heard only the voice, without echo. It arose in the mountain and thus did not bounce off it

—I swept my eyes over those garish slopes, once, twice, and three times. I turned away to rest my eyes, and then back, peering hard. And I saw the cave, a dark hole thirty or forty feet up, and I heard the voice again.

"Help!"

3.
The man who
was not a prince

He lay in the cave, dying. It did not take me long to realize that he had not yelled—after all, I should have known that any voice I heard here wouldn't yell for help in *English!*

Anyhow, it kept repeating, in my head as I subsequently learned, and I followed it. Yes, I was on the right track; it grew "louder" as I foozled my way up that mountain. Not, I am sorry to say, without scraping myself up pretty nicely.

But I made it, and entered that cave, dark and increasingly cool, and I found him. He lay on his back, his mouth ajar, and when I again "heard" him I realized that I was receiving his *thoughts:* his mouth did not move, nor did his thirst-thick tongue. He had repeatedly filled my mind with a picture begging succor. Now he projected another: he asked me either to kill him with the slim sword lying nearby, or to go further back into the cavern, where there was a spring-fed little stream. I brought the water, incidentally banging my head and scraping an elbow in the darkness of the cave.

Holding his head up, just a little, I gave him drink—just a little. It had obviously been quite awhile since he'd had water or anything else to drink, and I remembered having read that you should never overdo in such circumstances. It's easy to overdo, rescuing a patient from inanition. Now I know that his kind can go for long periods without water. Much longer than Earth people, me included. But that did not help my patient that first day here; he had passed his limit.

His leg was broken and he'd taken a nice wound low in the belly—or high in the intestine. It had bled a lot, all over his lower belly and genitals. He was stuck to the rock floor of the cave, in his own dried blood. When he moved, obviously with renewed life after receiving the water, his belly started leaking again.

He was a man. Whether his black hair grew that way or he'd shorn it, I couldn't be sure at the time, but it formed a manelike ridge along the center of his skull and on down his neck. A foot or so of it hung loosely from there down his back, like a beard hindside before. Like the scalplock of an American Indian —was it the Mohawks who wore that kind of hairdo? —the Mohicans? His brows were black, too, and his eyes, iris and all, so that they looked enormous, even though half-closed. There appeared to be no hair elsewhere on his body—except his face. He wore a rather wide but not bushy mustache, and a short beard that ran up his cheeks to the bottoms of his lobeless ears. No sideburns. No hair on his pate except for the scalplock.

The all-black eyes were strange, but I've seen people with eyes only a little different, their irises are so dark. And my father has no earlobes. And the hair— I'd no idea at the time if it just grew that way or if it had been shorn on either side, as a sort of decoration or tribal mark, like the Amerind hairdo it resembled.

The rest of it: two eyes, one mouth-type mouth, one nose, high-bridged and rather Italian-looking. Skin about the color of a penny. Not a shiny new penny; a year-old one, one that's been handled several times. The color of some of those exchange students

I'd seen from India, although a lot of them were considerably darker. As a matter of fact he bore a startling resemblance to a Delhi student I knew, Ram Gupta. A startling resemblance.

Two arms, two hands. Two legs (one very broken, and several days back, I thought). Each ended in a normal foot, shod in buskins of a blue-gray leather, laced with rawhide.

Normal. Standard homo sapiens type male. With standard reproductive equipment—stuck together with dried blood.

He'd worn flyless shorts, sort of like low-slung bikini briefs. Very tight, no more than straps on each hip, tied in a normal-looking knot. They were a jarringly bright red, apparently made of silk. Fire Island stuff. They'd been bright red even before he bled all over them. (I learned later that in back the job they made of covering him was only half-assed—literally.) He had stripped them off to bare his wound, but then hadn't been able to do anything about it.

And he wore that ancient, standard costume: a tunic, fancied up by being cut deep below the low, round neck and laced. It was made with only one sleeve, the left, embroidered with a yellow sword. The tunic was very short, and I saw that his briefs would still show if he stood. It was red, too, and apparently silk, with a little sheen.

He wore a broad baldric from left shoulder to right hip; it too was of blue-gray leather and supported both sword and dagger scabbards. He was left-handed. Mirror image?

His name was Kro Kodres. He was from someplace called Brynda, and he called this world "Aros." Big help. He had a message he was hot to get back to Brynda, but he'd been run down and chopped up by some inimical nomads called Vardors. Big help.

They left him for dead, taking his mount (a *slook*; big help again). He dragged himself up here, and now I had the explanations of the dark stains I'd seen on the rocks as I ascended. God, what stamina the man had!

He had no idea how long he'd lain here; several days, I could see that. And smell it. He was worried about a girl he'd stashed for safety: *cor* Jadiriyah. (I soon learned that "*cor*" means "the.")

He wanted to know who I was and where I was from. I told him, saw he didn't understand a word of it, and concentrated on thinking at him, as hard as I could. He frowned, poor Kro Kodres did, and began to look worried.

"Why do you shield your thoughts?" he asked, in my mind.

Rather than answer, I concentrated hard: *I'm not shielding my thoughts, I'm trying like all hell to broadcast!*

I failed; he didn't receive a thing. I learned it later, and I may as well say it now:

The people of Aros are telepaths: senders. That is, they don't "read minds," they broadcast their thoughts, so that others can "hear" them. It's purely voluntary, and they seldom use the ability save in times of stress; emergencies. And I should say "project" rather than broadcast. They've some astonishingly well-oiled machinery up there in their heads, and they can think *at* one person so that another nearby can't "hear" a thing. Anyhow, since they are only weak receiving sets with very powerful broadcasting equipment, all mental, and since I don't know how to broadcast, they can't hear a word I think.

"Hank Ardor," I said, touching my chest. "Hank Ardor."

"Hahnk Ahdah," he croaked, after several repetitions. Most of their *a*'s and *r*'s sound Bostonian, like Evelyn's, both pronounced "ah." Few people seem to pronounce *r*'s as most Americans do.

I smiled, nodding vigorously. "Hank Ardor," I said again, touching myself, and then touched his chest and said "Kro Kodres." He blinked in assent. If those people nodded, he couldn't have at the time.

"Where are you from?" he asked in my mind.

"America," I told him, and repeated it several times. He got it, but let me know he'd never heard of it, and hadn't seen much reddish hair either, and I didn't try to go any further. His clothing and weapons didn't look as if Copernicus or Galileo had showed up on Aros yet. It occurred to me that I might well shoot off my mouth about coming from the sky and get myself burned for a heretic, or whatever these people did to people who thought differently.

Kro Kodres had a knapsack of soft russet-colored leather. In it were implements, and a few coins, along with meat: jerked meat for a far traveler, but it tasted pretty good anyhow. I had a hunger. It is good otherwise, I will add, unless you don't like the meat you buy in kosher delicatessens. We had plenty of water, of course, from the shiveringly cool little stream in the back of the cave.

There seemed very little I could do for the poor guy, other than feed him, give him water, commiserate, and think positively. Set his leg?—could you? I didn't know anything about that, but I did see I'd have to break it again before I tried, anyhow. I didn't dare. Treat his wound? Sure. That's properly heroic, and I'd like to merit the image and say I performed brilliant medical rites over him. There was some powder in the knapsack, and he indicated that I should sprinkle his ripped gut with it. I did, but I didn't get much of anywhere. He was mostly dried blood there, and I figured that cruor was all that was holding him in—along with whatever blood he had left.

Bandage him up? All right, I did that. He wore little, and I nothing, but he did have a cloak, a long, heavy one that was white on one side and black on the other. Noticing that there seemed to be no particular inside or outside, I guessed the white would reflect the sun during the day. And—the black would disguise the wearer at night? The white contrasted nicely with his tunic and shorts, which looked like a sort of uniform, particularly with that embroidered design on the tunic sleeve.

Using his dagger—its back edge was saw-toothed; clever—I tore the cloak and bound him up around the middle as best I could. He started bleeding again, which gave me a fine helpless feeling as I secured the ends of the heavy cloth to make a tighter bandage. He seemed to appreciate it, and he tried to sit up with a little smile, and he passed out.

Shortly thereafter I learned something else about the planet Aros. It is warm by day, nearly all over save at the poles, of course, but where we were there was no humidity to boil us. Where we were, far from the equator, the temperature when I'd waked up here was probably a dry ninety degrees Fahrenheit. (I know centigrades are far more scientific and impressive, but it takes me about two minutes to convert each one.) But at night—well, I guess it dropped close to sixty. And that was damned cold, in a cave, without heat or clothing or covers, much less the pajamas I'd never worn anyhow.

Neither of us spoke the other's language, and we hadn't any books or paper or ball-points. But he

would say a word or phrase and project a picture
into my mind. Think about it: I got it fast, then faster, then I was rushing past the abecedarian stage, toward mastery of Aro, their language. It is used nearly
all over the planet, although of course there are
plenty of dialect and slang differences—and I've
never even been out of this hemisphere. Within
five days I was speaking pretty good pidjin Aro. Without his psi-broadcasting powers it'd have taken a
month just to get a noun vocabulary, without paper
and books. We didn't have a month. But we had
nothing else to do, and I'm good at languages, and
that vocal-plus-mental picture method is unbeatable.
It was almost like being programmed, force-fed.
All I had to do was remember.

He was very anxious about "the" Jadiriyah, but I
decided to hell with chivalry—I wasn't leaving him.
Maybe he'd heal, or the powder was magic, and he
and I could go for her together. Maybe he was a
prince, and Jadiriyah was his sister, and I'd be warlord, at the very least. I promised him I'd see about
her. Later. Yes, I'd be sure she got that odd ring. He
was mighty emphatic about that.

It's a good thing I stuffed myself with Aro in those
five days. Our supply of jerked meat was down to a
nubbin, I had a runny nose from night after cold
night (plus a bath in that icy stream), and—on the
fifth night Kro Kodres awoke me from the first sound
sleep I'd had. I knew why immediately. He was blister-
ing hot with fever, streaming sweat, and shivering
violently. He'd been twisting around; his bandages
were red-soaked and he was leaking through and beneath them.

"The golden cup is big bones!" he yelled, and he
yelled it again, struggling to get up. Then he collapsed,
and he died very quickly.

The poor guy was full of infection and he'd run out of blood to lose, and I'd been worse than useless to him.

I remembered the phrase: the golden cup is big bones! *"Hai azul thade cor zorveli nas!"* Although he'd run it together: *"Hai azulthade cor zorvelinas."*

You won't hear any valiant tales from me about how I buried him. Be properly shocked if you want, but— what's the use? If you're Christian or Jewish or one of several others, you think the body is nothing, a thing, a transitory chalice to hold the soul, which is going on alone—so why plant the body, other than as fertilizer for more bodies? In which case it shouldn't be neatly boxed anyhow. If you're from India and think you're coming back in a new body—as the Arones believe— then why bother with the old one? It's no more than a snake's discarded skin, a butterfly's cocoon. What's the market value of used cocoons?

No, we—I mean *you*, on Earth—plant people because they smell bad, and attract flies and animals and vultures and buzzards, and because a long long time ago our ancestors wanted the bodies of the faithful departed well-planted so they wouldn't come back and bug everybody. To be doubly certain, they piled rocks on top of the body-hole. Sure, that's why tomb-stones: remnant holdovers from when man used to heap rocks on graves, to keep the spirit down and out of his hair.

"The evil that men do lives long after them; the good is oft interred with the bones." So said Shake-speare (if the quotation's off, remember that I haven't anything here to crib from), and so our re-mote ancestors believed—literally. "Rest in peace" means just that: rest in peace down there, *don't get restless and come back; leave us in peace, too!* It's a command, not a well-wishing sendoff.

I left Kro Kodres lying on his back in the cave. How many stiffs got a private sepulcher with running water?

I left him there in his torn, blood-imbrued clothing, but without his weapons and gear and his (torn) cloak —and his buskins. (He had six toes. On each foot.) I performed the necessary but worse-than-unpleasant task of accepting the legacy of his boots and weapons, which I had to remove. I worked hard at washing everything in that cold stream, but some bloodstains remained. The water didn't do the leather baldric any good, either. His short, soft boots were a little wide in the feet and looser on my calves than his. I laced them tight and let my toes wander around in them.

From his cloak I made a loin-and-rump cover, sort of like an overgrown and particularly loose diaper. A thin strip from the same cloak served to belt the makeshift thing about me, low on my hips. There was no reason for anything else, so I slung the ragged remnant of his cloak around my shoulders as a sort of short mantle; it could also be pulled up to cover my head, if that sun tried boiling my brain.

I learned very soon what I *should* have done, and I expect you've already thought of it. I should have kept the cloak intact (except for the bandage I'd sliced and ripped out of it). It was long, and voluminous, and would have made me a sort of Bedouin burnūs, and I could have used it as a cover at night. But we of Earth have this thing about undergarments, and binding up our groins—shorts and briefs and even undershirts, in addition to all the female stuff. All totally unnecessary, most of the time, but I'm a briefs fan; I don't like swinging around loose.

Too, I admit I was not thinking too coherently just then. I was on an alien planet, in a cave, with a dead body for company. I did the first thing I half-thought of, which turned out to be a mistake.

Kro Kodres' water had been in a canteen attached to the saddle of his stolen mount. A quick test told me that his knapsack, well-made of one piece of leather, was watertight. That became my water sack. I dropped in the ring for Jadiriyah; it seemed the safest place. The few silver coins I tucked into the warm nook of my homemade shorts. Sooner or later, I'd probably need money. The fork and other tools I discarded.

He was chunkier, and I was taller.

I had to bore a new hole in his baldric to cinch the belt lower. That way the sword swung low on my right hip, for a fast crossdraw.

Perhaps I looked superbly exotic and heroic, like Frazetta or Jones artwork. Perhaps, in my black-and-white diaper made of a dead man's cloak, I looked more like a desipient clown. But I had clothes, and weapons I understood, and a little meat and several days' water, and a destination. I knew in which direction Kro Kodres' city of Brynda lay, and I knew where he'd left the girl Jadiriyah. First (the) Jadiriyah, then Brynda. I set out across the plain in my secondhand boots, chin high and eyes clear. It was going to be a long hike. After parking the girl, Kro Kodres had ridden many miles at a gallop, leading his pursuers away from her.

The orange alien sun beat down.

4.
The girl
I did not rescue

I walked for three days, hoping I had things straight and was heading in the right direction. I still couldn't see anything ahead but yellow plain becoming yellow sky, and I'm sure it was some sort of miracle that I found the pen. The gold Cross pen; Dr. Blakey's. It was twinkling in the dust, and it had his initials on it —sort of: ꟻᗡB

Reversed, just like me. Why?

I slung it around my neck on one of several raw-hide thongs from Kro Kodres' pack. I plodded on. No, I'll relieve you of wondering; I didn't see that stupid parrot—then. All I found was yellow plain streaming out to merge into yellow sky, with boulders and clouds scattered here and there. I ate the last collop of my meat the evening of the second day, and by the following noon I was beginning to think of Kro Kodres. I hadn't buried him—why hadn't I broken another taboo and brought him along?

—Or part of him?

That charming and unwonted thought made me sick, and I dry-heaved for awhile, trudging on, deciding I wouldn't have been able to eat the poor bugger anyhow.

The short sword had gotten a good deal heavier. So had the knapsack containing my water supply, although it was only half-full now. I learned my first lesson about what I should have done with that cloak very quickly: the baldric chafed my bare skin. I made

some adjustments, to pad the strap, looking even
more makeshift and clownish. Lesson number two I
learned that first night: I longed for the whole cloak
to cover up with. I'd have been better off traveling at
night and sleeping by day, stopping to curl up in the
shadow of some big rock. There were quite a few,
and some were house-size. I know and admit now
what I *should* have done, about several matters. I
just didn't think about them at the time. I'm afraid
I'm just not John Carter.

You have a choice: you can stick with me, a rea-
sonably tough incompetent, with admittedly more
pluck than sense, or you can just forget it and go back
to the supermen-heroes. I'm not an antihero, at least.

For three days I saw no sign of life. For three nights
I slept in the dust—it wasn't quite as cold as the cave,
but it tried.

Late in the second day I learned why a plain like
this is called a "trackless" waste; lord knows I was
leaving tracks your Aunt Nellie could follow, by touch.
But that afternoon a breeze came up. It was lovely—
for awhile. Then it gained strength, and next I knew I
could see absolutely nothing in the insane swirl of
choking yellow dust. Squatting down right in the
middle of it, I soaked my torn "mantle" with water
and tied it around my face. Then I staggered on, remembering I'd been heading directly for a collection
of several close-set boulders. I kept my eyes closed;
they were no good in that dust storm anyhow, except
for collecting dust.

I ran into the boulders—literally—and fell among
them, again, literally. I lay there and kept my eyes
shut and tried to keep breathing wet, used air. It
lasted a long time. Perhaps two or three hours; I
had no watch, then.

It died, fortunately, before I did, leaving me covered with dust. Covered. I spanked off about a ton of it, leaving only a truckload or so. I considered washing it off, but I was afraid to. I might have a far more pressing need for my scantling supply of water, and if I found Jadiriyah I'd have to share it. I walked on, ignoring the sun's bloody setting, and kept on through the cooler night until I collapsed. I slept until the sun nudged me awake.

That third evening I found Jadiriyah.

But the Vardors found her first.

Toward sunset I was plodding hungrily along, and for fully an· hour I watched a moving dust cloud. I had no idea how far away it was, or what was causing it. It had a definite matrix, and trailed only a slowly-settling wake. That made me decide it was a moving something or someone, rather than another big wind. After an hour or so (?) it seemed·to swerve toward me. I measured the distance to my goal: a collection of rocks marked by a couple of Cadillac-sized boulders set close together like stone lovers. I speeded up. They were hours away. Then I realized the dust cloud and I shared the same goal.

The dust cloud kept rolling, ghostlike. I could hear the pounding of hooves. Then the cloud was on the opposite side of the cluster of rocks, and I could see only its tenuous upper portions. It reached the rocks long before I did; the rocks where I was supposed to find the Jadiriyah.

It was as if I were listening to an invisible radio —with earplugs. The sound was in my head, not in the air. I saw flickering images, too, and they were only in my head. I kept moving wearily, tuned in to the weird drama. In stress, she was broadcasting desperately.

*I heard a thought, but it was garbled—it isn't Kro
Kodres! The thought was deliberately damped; these
riders are not friends! I slide in between the biggest
boulders, which are about three feet apart. I draw my
sword. My heart is like thunder in my chest; my
breasts heave and I am suddenly wet with perspira-
tion. I fill my left hand with dagger-hilt.*

*They pound up and stop ten or so paces away in a
great cloud of swirling xanthic dust, and we all wait
for it to dissipate. I see them.*

(I saw them through *her* mind; *she* recognized them.
I didn't. They weren't horses, and their riders weren't
Kro Kodres' people. They were enough to bring on
the jimjams.)

The horse-sized beasts were a dark grayish blue, like
some earthly cats. Their heads resembled foxes far
more than cats or horses, with long thin snouts and
entirely too many teeth. They had no manes. Their
ears were floppy and their tails stubby, though
equipped with the usual whisk broom ends big animals need to swat flies. [Yes, there are. God was
just as overgenerous with flies on Aros as he was on
Earth. An obvious error in the Grand Design.] The
beasties' feet were huge, splayed for desert travel, and
yellow, for no good reason other than decor. Foot
fetishists, maybe. Oh, one other thing about those
feet: there were six of them. Something for a fet-
ishist to get his teeth into!

The riders were blue-gray, rather than gray-blue
like their mounts. Hairless, as I learned, although
when I first saw them, through *her* eyes, they wore
long white robes with cowls, like Arab burnūses. Their
noses were huge and broad, resembling a gorilla's
more than anything, with long-slitted nostrils. The
mouths: gashes, hardly any lip at all. The teeth: hu-

man enough, a little animalish. Yellow eyes, with hazel irises and tiny pupils. They were set very deep. Not as different as the green men and other creatures we've all read about, but different enough, I assure you. They were not quite human; they were very alien; they were staring at her with those deepset, teeny-tiny black pupils. She was a lonesome, scared female.

Besides, they were eight feet tall, give or take a few centimeters.

They wore boots beneath those loose-sleeved robes —boots obviously made from the beasts they rode (slooks, of course). A shortish bow was slung on the back of each rider, with arrows on his saddle. Each wore a sword girded on with a thick sash. The robes were white; the sash of one was orange, the other's an eye-rending chartreuse.

"Put down your steel, Kang-she," the thought came, murkily, relayed. "We have bows and need to come no closer."

I shake my head. They look at each other, white cowls twisting ghostily in the twilight. Twilight is bloody red, on bloody Aros. *One of them unlimbers his bow. The other argues, with a lot of gesticulating.*

"I am Jadiriyah of Brynda," I say, "and desire only to be allowed to go in peace, unless you offer aid. I have nothing of value, not even a mount."

You're right: She should've told them Daddy and Hubby and forty thousand knights of the Table Round were just over yonder. She probably would have, too, if she'd thought of it! These were Vardors, the not-quite-human nomads who'd attacked Kro Kodres. They'd rather raid and fight and slay and rape than eat or sleep. They'd hardly offer aid to each other, much less her; she was a she of the Kang race,

and the races were natural enemies, theirs and Kro
Kodres'. As to giving her a ride—sure they would!
Straight to hell, or to Vardor slavery, which is about
the same difference.

I began to bounce forward, seven-league-boots
style. I had done very little of it in my three days'
traveling. True, it eats up the distance. But despite the
fact that I could leap *far*, I was still jumping. Just
how long do you think you'd last if you tried to make
a journey by *jumping?* Whether you could spring
three feet or thirty wouldn't make much difference.
You'd still wear yourself out, and need a lot of two
commodities I didn't have in addition to rest: food
and water.

I was already gasping. I knew I wouldn't make it.
They were regarding her in silence, their homely, gray
faces shadowed and sharp-etched by their cowls.

*"You have much of value," the one still wearing his
bow on his back says in a growly voice, and my spine
writhes. He laughs. "This idiot would spoil it with an
arrow. Not Ard," he says, thumbing his robed chest.
"I am not so stupid as Oth. Put down your weapons. We will share food with you, and perhaps help
you on your way, if it does not take us out of ours."*

*Our bluffs cross like swords. There is no way out.
We cannot part in peace, having seen each other. Besides, I am female, on foot, and armed only for close
combat, while they have mounts and arrows. I wait,
wondering if they will decide to shoot, to come in for
me on slookback, or dismount and take me from
either side. It makes little difference. I have no
place to go and cannot hope to overcome two of
them. Kro Kodres has the Ring; Kro Kodres is not
coming, although I broadcast, just in case.*

They swing down and start in, Oth ("oath") going

*around one boulder to come at me from the opposite
direction. They will try to take me alive. After all, as
Ard said, I have much of value. Why am I too weak
to slay myself?*

*I startle Ard by advancing, sword and dagger
ready. He blinks at my bravura, raising his own blade.
I show him a trick or two, learning quickly that I am
better with a sword than he.*

These people, I saw in my mind, had barely begun
any scientific sword-to-sword defense. Besides, when
you're eight feet tall and about one-third animal, you
rely more on size and strength than on brains and
dexterity. But just as she started to settle down, smiling, to carve up the monster, she heard the other Vardor behind her. She played the only card she had.
Not an ace maybe, but it was at least a queen against
that pair of jacks! She charged. Taken aback, he
dodged her extended blade, and she rushed past,
listening to their echoed cries. For a moment they
were so dumbstruck that they stood and stared with
open mouths, rather than rushing after her.

Which was when I stumbled and fell sprawling.
Lying there gasping, I found I could not rise. I was
exhausted. What use would I be to that gutsy girl anyhow, in this condition? I hadn't even the breath to
yell. No, I'd be dead in a moment. I realized what
I had to do: lie there. If she escaped—wonderful. If
she didn't—well, they didn't intend killing her anyhow. I'd have to let them have her, while I tried to
get up enough strength to reach those rocks and be
of some value. Besides, it was coming on for darkness. They'd use her, and then sleep.

And then I'd move in. One hungry, exhausted man
against two monsters has to think sensibly, heroic or
not, like it or not. Playing Galahad, rushing in as I

had been before the fall knocked some sense into me, would have accomplished exactly zero. One dead hero.

Meanwhile she was racing for their mounts. Howling, the Vardors started loping after her. She was going to make it! She had a foot up into the stirrup of Oth's slook, grasping the big saddle horn with one hand. No go; she had to pause and sheath her sword, and I sweated with her as she grabbed that saddle horn with both hands. She swung up and into the great bucket of a saddle, seized the beast's reins, and pulled on one of them, telling him to vamoose.

All this I saw through her eyes, and I felt her elation as she could not feel mine: she was going to make it.

She didn't. What made that miserable gray beasty stop? It was days later that I learned: slooks, too, receive the projected thoughts of the people of Aros. And his master told him to stop and get the hell back. Confused, the slook dug in his forehooves, then his middle set, dragging, as is the way of slooks, the extra long back legs. Very efficient braking mechanism. Her brain registered the report of her ears: hooves drumming after her. Desperately she kicked the animal.

At last he started forward, yielding to physical commands rather than vocal or mental ones: they hurt more. But he had hesitated just long enough, and that pause made a tremendous change in both her life and mine.

Ard was alongside her, at the gallop. Without ever having seen a western movie in his life, he jumped.

She whoofed and tried to cling to the reins as his robed body crashed into hers. But Ard's weight and

impact were already toppling her from the saddle,
and she released the reins as she—and I, in my mind
—felt them start to cut into her/my fingers. She hung
onto her sword, hoping she wouldn't manage to cut
herself with it when she l

                        a
                          n
                        d
                          e
                        d
                          !

My mind felt the jar as hers did. With a heavy
impact and a groan, both heightened by Ard's weight.
The monster fell on top.

*We do not roll. He merely lies atop me, on my
back. His arms are a vise about my waist: pain. I
gasp for breath, striving to get at my dagger. The
sword is useless in this situation, but perhaps I can
stab back . . . I gain the dagger hilt—and Ard exerts
more strength in a lurch. Pain! My head roars. My
eyes pop. Pain. I am sure ribs crack. I cannot breathe.
Consciousness is failing. My fingers are as if mittened,
scrabbling at the hilt of my knife.*

*Ard releases me! I suck in all the air I can—drag
out my dagger—Ard is pushing back from me. He is
swinging a blow against the side of my hea—*

5.
The girl who
was not Dejah Thoris

I won't try to keep you in suspense, or pretend that some miracle occurred, or that I valiantly dragged myself up, bounded in one mile-long leap to them, and chopped both of them into Vardor sausage. There was no miracle. No Aronian god popped out of the machine and intervened. I remained where I was, lying sprawled on the yellow desert. Through her mind, I "listened."

Ard had brought her down; Ard took his turn first. When she came to she was on her back in that soft yellow dust, her arms pulled up and back. The other Vardor, Oth, was holding them tight against the ground, which did not come close to requiring all his strength. Her legs were unfettered, as if that were of any value to her: the pain that awakened her was that of Ard's entry. Apparently he accomplished it in about the same way mostly newly-wed American husbands do (or did—you people grown up yet? Did the Freedom to Read of the Sixties help any?). Violently, suddenly, quickly, and totally without finesse or regard for her. Just do it and assume with o'erweening masculine ego that she's loving every minute of it.

Which, as it turned out, Arone women do.

If Jadiriyah had been a maiden, she no longer had to worry about being snatched by unicorn hunters. Under a sky containing one big yellowish moon and, far across the heavens, another smaller one, I "witnessed"—*experienced*—a scene I'd only read about and seen—carefully presented. Ard had his Kang woman. Sprawled on my face on an alien planet, wallowing in soft dust (as she was, but on her back), I experienced all of it with the Jadiriyah. Rummaged by one eight-foot andromorph with blue-gray skin while his partner held her, she joined the ranks of girls who've had the experience without a hint of love. (About six-tenths, on Earth, except in California where it's maybe eight-tenths. Here on Aros it's closer to 9.99.)

I—*I!*—felt a jagged spear of pain, another—and then a slackening of it, a dull hurt that faded slowly as she wallowed, crushed into dust that was soft but highly unyielding. She had cried out as she awoke. Now she pressed her lips tight and lay as still as possible, trying to still her groans. Eight-foot Vardors are built proportionately big all over.

Yell? She would not. That would have increased his pleasure: violence comes natural to all us males, including the blue-gray almost-men of Aros. Wiggle? Try to throw him off? Buck, try to twist away? She knew better. That is known as passion, and is reserved for situations in which the woman is a participant, not an object. It's women who are still and quiet who create unhappy husbands and get written about in articles in psychology journals and the women's magazines. (There, I mean, on Earth; we are forced to struggle along without *Family Circle* and Helen Girlie Brown here.)

The Jadiriyah lay still and quiet. And felt it, broadcasting with tremendous power. Perhaps I'll go into Arone Frequency-modulation (mental) later.

Well, she was not quite still. I was very conscious, as her brain was, of her one anxious movement. I was astonished at it, astonished that she could think of such at such a time. Where was her horror? Where was the shrieking anguished shock and revulsion and horror that traumatizes American girls in similar circumstances, some into amnesia or catatonia or the male-hating lesbianism that is a sort of catatonia?

Absent. She was not exactly overjoyed at this penile penetration in which she was far from a willing participant, but she accepted it with singular aplomb. Her prime thought was to gain all possible clitoral stimulation. She succeeded, and my astonishment grew: she was there at the peak before Ard was!

Had I been in any doubt about being on a planet other than Earth, the reservations would have vanished then.

It was over very soon, and he was lying on her/me/us, even heavier in the gasping ennui of his exhaustion. "I" felt the pain lessen as his hugeness diminished and he sighed wearily: *post coitam omnia anima triste est,* someone said a long time ago, but it's more tired than sad.

There was another flash of pain as he pushed back, regarded her for a moment, smiling, then rose to his knees and stood. He went to relieve his companion Oth at her arms. I gritted my teeth, trying to prepare myself for the Jadiriyah's broadcast of the next oversized invader.

He comes, with some pain, though less than the other one. I clamp my mouth tight. He is even huger than Ard. The pain is less, now, but it hurts. He is so heavy! But I shed no tears. Perhaps I will weep later, if they do not slay me. If I am to be slain I shall not give them the satisfaction of my tears! I regret the cry they've already heard from me. Kro Kodres would have been better than this. Easier and less painful.

He is big, but not Vardor-huge—where is he? Could they have caught him? Could these be the same ones who pursued him, after he left me here to lead them off and return to take his pleasure later? Perhaps he is dead! Mixed emotions . . . he deserves no less than death, but . . . if he is, then I have no hope of rescue, no hope ever of seeing Brynda again! And all the time I have waited here!

Unh—! He batters me, this beast, like the clapper of a great bell rung by a madman. But . . . I cannot be still . . . ah, that's good! Such an effort; he is concentrating on himself, not me, but I am sure he is trying not to pleasure me—which takes effort on his part, the monster! Ah . . . good . . . good . . . it rises, like water, warm water . . . flowing up . . . over me . . . enveloping me . . . aAHHHHHHH!

She arrived, and then he did, and then I did, helplessly. Sprawled on my belly, I could only groan and strive to grind myself into the satiny dust. My diaper-like briefs, I thought, would be stiff tomorrow.

The Vardor, his business finished, slid back. He pushed himself to his knees and looked down at the girl. Cursing her for an unresponsive, frozen Kanganimal, he slapped her so that her head rang—and I grunted and listened to the ringing in my own skull. She became aware of the headache left her by the previous blow from Ard. Then her nocturnal ravagers stood over her, side by side, and laughed.

They had opened a Kang-she. Now they pretended contempt; Oth kicked her in the side, just between hip and ribs, and they watched her twist, trying to fold up. They laughed the louder.

Then they turned her over and wiped her face in the dust until she gasped and then sneezed several times running, floundering and writhing—while they laughed.

"She tries to blow the powerful spirit of our life juice out her nose," Oth exulted, "so that she'll not bear two fine Vardors."

I've never killed anyone, I thought. *But I swear I think carving Oth up might be fun!*

They bound her wrists behind her back with a raw-hide strip that was entirely too thin. I felt its bite as she did. They also indulged in a little fondling while she lay there silently enduring it. I was shocked at what I saw in her mind: they died horribly, both of them, horribly and slowly and very bloodily indeed. In her mind. *Well,* I thought, *that sort of experience could make a woman that bloodthirsty, I suppose. I believe it has me.*

Stretching out on their saddle blankets on either side of her, they went calmly to sleep. Both slept on their backs, and her mind broadcast disgust at their snores. I listened carefully, striving to cock my ears in that silent Arone night. But I heard nothing; I was too far away. And it was time. I started dragging myself to my feet. I tried to think of what would *not* taste good; I could think of nothing. Even a bagel would have tasted palatable to me then. And I think I could have slept on a bed of nails.

She astonished me again, although I thought I'd been shocked, surprised, astounded, etc. etc. so many times already by her mind and behavior I was numb. This time she went to sleep, quite soon after they did. Oh sure, she tested her bonds first.

I dragged myself up and moved in. I was weak from hunger, but rested, at least. The rocks grew larger and larger as I approached.

Just as I reached them, over an hour later, Jadiriyah's mind came alive again in mine (no, her dreams were not broadcast). Oth was waking her, pulling her to him. This time it was worse. Her hands dug into her back and the rawhide thongs cut into her wrists; I could feel them.

Suddenly I wondered: why had I never felt Kro Kodres' pain? Was this woman's mind so powerful? She had "told" me, of course; she was "broadcasting," in hopes K.K. would hear and come arunning.

She groaned. I heard her in my ears, not in my brain. Instantly he slapped one hand over her mouth and clamped the other around her upper arm, glancing at the still-sleeping Ard and giving her a dangerous look.

So *he does not want his comrade wakened*, she thought. *He removes his paw from my lips—*

I *heard* her scream, aurally and mentally, and I started violently, fearful I'd given away my presence. No, they were all too busy. She howled and did her best to hurl herself into orbit. I had just started forward. I halted. *Damn* her! Now she had them both awake. Oth had been about eight seconds away from getting my sword in his back; I figured it would take no longer than that to cover the twenty or so feet separating them from me.

Now I could see them. The girl barely; little more than an arm, her soles, glimpses of her legs. His back was toward me. Even in the moonlight I could see his color. Slate, dirty slate.

Ard came awake just as Oth belted her one across the face—it hurt, and this time automatic tears squirted. The tears angered her. But Ard wasn't mad. He laughed and told his friend—if Vardors have "friends" in the sense we do (do *we?*)—to hold up a bit. Roll back on your side, Oth. Attaboy—pull her with you. Fine, now I'll . . . oop, her tied hands are in the way. (He rectified that with his dagger, separating her wrists.) There. Now put your hands on Oth's hips, Kang-she, and keep them there unless you want your head crushed like a jubb-egg!

That was the gist of what he said, in a voice like gravel rolling across old leather. She obeyed. She wound up gripping Oth's hips until he groaned; she had to have something to clutch. This time she was not groaning, or cooperating. She was screaming, screaming in a hideous voice that sounded as though she were stripping the lining from her throat.

I winced, wishing fervently that I could tune her out. She shrieked. Louder than ever before in her life, if her brain remembered correctly, because she'd never really felt pain before in her life, until then. She'd only thought she had.

I shared her pain, and I stopped considering and watching and being careful. I eased out Kro Kodres' sword and took a deep breath and another and crouched, low. Then I leaped. Soared. I drifted down, I struck, jackknifing my legs. I leaped again: over twenty feet in two bounds, the first from a standing start.

Ard was groaning and hunching, yowling to Oth about the felicities of this dual activity with the soft Kang-she. He sounded as if she were a game of Monopoly they were playing for the first time. He laughed—

—And I was there, coming lightly down only a couple of feet behind him, swinging my sword while I was still airborne. It took only one blow: I swung that good Arone sword like a woodman attacking a Sequoiah. It chopped into his gray back just at the base of his neck, slicing through the pad of flesh there between his shoulders. And on in. When the blow at last dissipated itself—with a shocking jolt to my arm—his head was attached to his big trunk only by part of his trachea, a few shreds of flesh, and perhaps a leader or two.

His body, jerking ever harder now, did not fall back. His hands clutched the girl in the spasmodic grip of sudden death and its gamic release known to hangmen everywhere.

I could still see very little of her, and little more of Oth. But his face was there, peering at me over her shoulder with very wide eyes, and I dragged the sword out of his companion and shoved it into the right eye. His shriek drowned hers. His hands, of course, did not clutch her the tighter, but snapped reflexively up to his face. He fell back from her. I dropped a hand to the shoulder of the jerking, blood-spouting chunk of dead meat that had been Ard. Dragging him back, I also pulled the girl. Away from Oth.

I stepped across her and, aiming carefully, thrust between Oth's upraised arms. The blade went in, and I leaned on it. But it did not seem to kill him, and I pulled it out and stabbed him again. Then I stepped back, satisfied he was dying or dead. I didn't give a damn which.

It had been a very brief fight. It had not, in point of fact, been a fight at all. I merely charged in and killed two men—almost-men. My first two. Obviously I could have shouted, to give them an opportunity to disengage themselves from their victim and seize their weapons so that we could have had a "fair fight." But that sort of twisted concept of fair play is also known as "suicide." I could also have said *something*, to allow Ard to turn and see his death as it came, rather than merely chopping him in the back.

But if a man is to kill, and he knows, what difference does it make whether the killee knows and sees it coming, or gets it in the back? None, save this: backstabbing is much less cruel. Ard, for instance, very literally never knew what hit him. *He* died, come to think, in a moment of ecstatic joy.

"Blackie!" the TV or movie hero snaps, and Blackie spins and the hero blasts him into the next world. It appeals to the American idea of fair play, that sort of fiction—and to American sadism.

Because it was far more kind to put that slug in Blackie's back and be done with it, without giving him that instant of horror.

(Also safer. Had it been Blackie who'd snapped "Whitehat!" the hero would not have spun and died. He'd have dived sideways, behind a horse trough or something, and Blackie's fate would have been the same. But I've always had that terrible thought: those villains are usually pretty clever. In reality, wouldn't *they* dive behind a horse trough?)

Both Ard and Oth jerked and kicked and thrashed quite a bit, but I had stabbed one three times and sheared off the other's head but for a few strings, and their movements were the reflexes of death. Blood had spurted hotly up my arm. Both of them bled on the girl. But she rolled over and looked curiously at me, ignoring the gore and the thrashing and the noises.

She had more aplomb than I; I turned away and walked about three steps before I dropped to both knees and vomited. Or tried to, dry-heaving convulsively and painfully as my belly strove to empty itself of its contents: nothing.

After a minute or two of that embarrassing unpleasantness I dragged myself to my feet and turned back to her.

She looked familiar. She was a good-looking woman, with a mass—a very tangled mass, now—of blue-black hair and black eyes beneath long lashes and a petulant mouth above a slightly dimpled chin. Straight, British-looking nose. Broad shoulders, supporting a swelling chest which my American eyes picked out very quickly. Blood had splashed on one, I forget which, and was dripping as if someone had injected red dye into a nursing mother. Her belly was round rather than flat, and so were her hips and thighs; she was thick, I guess, if you're particularly fond of, say, Nancy Sinatra types.

I was, but I'd always felt that that witch's mirror on the wall would have to reply: "Sophia's the fairest, dummy! Who else?"

The Jadiriyah sat back, legs widespread and outstretched, her hands behind her, serving as props. There was quite a bit of blood on her, although as far as I knew none of it was her own.

"Who are you?"

The words are "Thank you, Sir Knight, for rescuing me, albeit a trifle late," I thought, but I said, "Hank Ardor." I brandished my bloodstained sword. "And this belonged to Kro Kodres. You are Jadiriyah of Brynda?"

She looked down at herself. "Ugh!" She raised her eyes to me again, nodding. "Yes. You've slain Kro Kodres?"

"I found him dying. In a cave, three days' walk from here." I nodded to indicate which way; how did I know what direction was which? I'd seen no moss, and for all I knew Aros' orange sun rose in the west—or for the matter of that the south.

"He summoned me there, with his mind, but I could barely hear him, even though I was close by.

He'd taken a wound, here." I touched my lower belly. "And his leg was broken."

"Well, Hahnk Ahdah, I suppose now you'll claim your compensation."

"My what?"

"Your reward!" she said, her tone conveying "what else, clod?" The word she used was "julan," which translates as either reward or compensation. Kro Kodres hadn't explained well enough, and so I paid for my too-little understanding of her language and customs. I paid pretty dearly.

"I—"

"Well?" She cocked her head.

"Uh—nothing necessary, ma'am," I said. How do you make a *beau geste*, be a nice guy here, *without* being corny? I smiled, in best unassuming hero Gary Cooper fashion.

She looked at me, and I swear there seemed to be anger in her eyes—but it was gone, and she nodded. Anger that I hadn't demanded a reward? Maybe there was something I didn't know. But—too late now.

I put that from my mind, but I was frowning, too: "Why don't I hear you in my mind, now?"

"I'm not send—" She gazed at me intently, then frowned. The frown deepened. Suddenly I realized: she was "listening."

"I can't *hear* you!" (The word is "silgor," from "gorin," mind, and "silek, silethe," to read.)

I should have lied. I should have pretended a great ability to mask my thoughts. I didn't think of it, then. I was unaware of any reason to dissemble with her, and I am not much of a liar anyhow.

"A blow on the head," I said, choosing the lesser lie, the natural one. One doesn't go about introducing oneself as a visitor from another planet, after all. Not if one has anything resembling sense.

"A blow on the head made you unable to mind-speak?"

I nodded.

"Ugh! It must be worse than blindness! Ugh!" She shivered, shaking her head. But then: "Did Kro Kodres give you anything for me?"

What a woman! Acted a little insulted because I claimed no reward. Didn't say thanks. Then asked calmly if I had anything for her, sitting there with the two dead creatures stiffening at our feet. Their presence, by the way, didn't seem to disturb her in the least, any more than the blood on her body. "Ugh," she'd said, that was all; as if she'd looked in the mirror and seen that her hair was coming undone. She had accepted my brief statement about Kro Kodres' death, again with nothing resembling emotion or remorse. She did not *sympathize* with my "affliction," she merely thought how awful it would be. Now she asked, calmly and conversationally, if he had given me anything for her. Without a word, even the usual hollow words, of sympathy or—*something*.

And she hadn't thanked me. Nor was she making any effort to close her legs.

To call her a strange woman would be to say that Einstein was a bright fellow. I was shaken. I still am, a bit, thinking back on it. But there's no use piling up nouns and adjectives and superlatives: she was the strangest human being I'd ever encountered. I suppose she still is. Of course now I've some idea why. At that time—at that time she was obviously tough, and thus far she'd neither done nor said anything I expected.

And . . . she looked . . . familiar.

"Uh—yes," I said. "A ring, and a message." I wondered if the message was for her. He had never said.

Her eyes sparkled. "Save the message—where is the ring?"

"Uh—" I glanced at the Vardor mounts. Saw the waterbags, fat, nearly full. I nodded and unstrapped mine and dumped it out on the ground. The ring rattled in the neck, then plopped into the dust. I started to bend for it.

And a slender, strong-looking hand shot out and snatched it up. I looked up in fresh surprise; she had got up and come over without a sound or a flicker to apprise me that she was other than still sprawled atween the corpses. And she'd grabbed that ring as if it were Kidd's long-lost treasure. I straightened, watching her.

She looked even better standing. She was the kind of a girl that a man first sees nude and immediately thinks she looks as good or better that way as clothed, which is of course always a mistake. She was as close to perfect as a woman can get without being ridiculous about it, despite the fact that she was dirty, and blood-splashed, and stringy-haired. I wondered what she'd look like clean and brushed and ready for the boudoir, and I had a hard time trying to visualize improvements. I knew she'd be spectacular, clothed. Dazzling. She was, even now.

Her teeth flashed in a smile, and her eyes sparkled delightedly. She had her precious ring.

Later I wished I'd done a little bartering with that precious ring!

Blood—Vardor blood—trickled slowly from her, unnoticed now as she drew the ring on her finger—the left index. She held it up, smiling, her eyes flashing black jewels full of . . . avarice? Call it ineffable delight.

Those black eyes rose to me. That petulant mouth stretched in a grin—yes, a grin, not a smile. Again, my mind flickered a light along its hallways; she looked familiar. But there wasn't time to think about that:

"Ah, that feels better. Now I am whole! You have clothing, and plenty of food and water," she nodded at the saddlebags near the hobbled slooks, "and both mount and pack animal. Well! Good fortune, Hank Ahdah!"

And she closed her right hand over the left, folding down thumb and all fingers save that on which the odd ring glittered. She closed her eyes.

"Brynda," she murmured.

And she vanished.

6.
The girl who
was Elizabeth Taylor

I stood there and stared through the spot where Jadiriyah had been. Stupid; she wasn't coming back. I'd saved her life (or at least saved her from Vardor servitude), not to mention the traditional fate worse than which death isn't. (That she had apparently not been entirely discommoded by her ravishment is beside the point, surely. It *was* rape.)

She hadn't thanked me. She'd just—I reconstructed. Yes, I had it right the first time. She'd just rubbed the ring she'd snatched from me and—disappeared.

So it was a magic ring. So I'm an American, and I don't *believe* in magic. Didn't. Apparently it was time to start.

I had rescued the fair maiden in distress, and not only was she presumably not the daughter of the planetary ruler, she was an ungrateful bitch. And a vanishing witch. And I had thought *all* damsels in distress were princesses and their saviors became warlords, emperors, kings—princes at the very least!

I sat down. (I didn't decide to. My legs did.) I looked around, and up, and around again. Aros. I had now met two Arones, unless one counted Vardors—I didn't, and don't. Kro Kodres had not (at least so I assumed) been a prince or anything of the sort. I wasn't even certain if the poor guy had been a warrior; maybe he was a courier. Packing a ring belonging to a witch—whose face had seemed vaguely familiar.

I squinted my eyes, then closed them, trying to call up a mental picture of the girl whose face I'd seen so briefly. (And at that, not under the best conditions: it was night, she was dirty, and her hair was a mess.) Besides, she was naked, so that I didn't study her face much. I couldn't evoke her image. She couldn't look familiar: *I must be déjà-vuing,* I thought. *I probably have a mental picture of her from K.K.'s mind, and from hers. That makes me think she's familiar.*

Having thus handily disposed of the most minor of the mysteries, I opened my eyes again. Back to Kro Kodres. One: not royalty.

Two: he was carrying a message. He'd forgot to tell me who it was for. Maybe for Miss bitchwitch Jadiriyah, who hadn't given me time to deliver it. I repeated it to make sure I still had it: *Hai azul thade cor zorveli nas.* Yeah: the golden cup is big bones. OK. I still had that. So what?

Three: I'd killed the two Vardors. I glanced over at them. Ugh. Don't let anybody kid you. A stiff is a stiff, and they're all bad stuff. True, some are worse than others. Like: those two. Not just that they were gray, and too tall; they were all over blood, and I was not a man who'd seen a lot of blood. As a matter of fact I couldn't remember having seen any other than my own, in any quantity worth mentioning. Oh —and all that red stuff in the Peter Cushing movies, but I hardly counted that.

I stood up. Well, I thought, I'm in possession of two good riding slooks, food (how could I have forgotten how hungry I was?), water, a good-sized munitions dump—their weapons, Kro Kodres', and Jadiriyah's. And clothing: what I wore and, again, the Vardors' and—hers. She'd departed in the same state she'd been in when I had come belatedly bounding to the rescue: bare.

I packed up everything there was, mounted one slook, hung onto the reins of the other, and got the hell away from there.

No, I did not bury them, either. Why should I try to cheat buzzards, jackals, or whatever?

I ate as I rode. An hour or so later I halted, made sure my Arone beasties were all hobbled, and I stretched out. I was asleep in about seventeen seconds.

None of it made any more sense in the morning. As a matter of fact it made less, because I awoke knowing who the Jadiriyah looked like. My subconscious had been ferreting about through my memory banks while I lay asleep, and proudly it produced its catch as the sun awoke me.

She looked like Elizabeth Taylor. Pre-Cleopatra, pre-Burton Taylor, when she was slenderer. I had not been able to place that face and body at once because: *first,* the circumstances: one doesn't expect to wind up on a planet way the hell someplace or other and run into Elizabeth Taylor! (Don't get excited; figure of speech. She WASN'T Taylor; she just looked like her. As it turned out later, when I saw her properly clothed and cosmeticized and coiffed, she looked *exactly* like that most unique sex symbol: the one who could act. *second:* her state of deshabille, just mentioned. *third:* she looked like our Liz years ago, not as she was when I left you, just after having seen THE SECRET CEREMONY and noticing that the two female stars in it could have profited by swapping twenty-five carefully-chosen pounds.

Which, of course, reminded me that Kro Kodres had resembled—quite strongly—that beturbanned Indian I'd gone to school with, Ram Gupta.

Maybe, I thought, *this is one of those alternate*

Earths I've read about. Which could raise problems: what if I meet me? Oh—I guess he's back on my Earth.

Or maybe it's what passes for heaven, and I died in that machine of Dr. Blakey's. I hadn't seen Ram Gupta for several months. *Maybe Ram was in a car accident or something, and he's dead too.* (At which point I had an uncharitable thought: *Serves 'im right! That'll teach him to hang around America because it's nicer, rather than take his education back home to Delhi where they need him!*)

There was a flaw in that one: if this was "Heaven," how come he'd died here? And what about the Vardors, even if Liz Taylor HAD got killed or died just after my departure from Earth?

I could think of several flaws in the alternate or parallel Earth theory, too, including the parrot Dr. Blakey had sent. How come his replacement hadn't shown up back "home," if this was a swap deal? And if it wasn't . . . if there was another Hank Ardor here, and another Pope Borgia . . . then weren't we two objects occupying the same space at the same time? A paradox in Aristotle's logical universe?

Both were wild theories. Trouble is, now I know the truth, it is no less wild. It also contains paradoxes.

But when I woke up that morning on the yellow desert I hadn't the foggiest where I was, other than—someplace else.

I lay there awhile, trying to asimilate it, toying with the two look-alikes I'd met. And reviewing Jadiriyah's clothing or lack of same, which led me to Kro Kodres', and the Vardors—who had worn standard desert garb. Which I now wore.

Despite nature-addicts and -ists, clothing is important for more than cover and what some idiots call "morality." Clothing is also decoration, adornment.

The first clothing was probably nothing more. It was becoming so again when I left America, and would become even more so with environmental control—and assuming the country didn't become totally Pastoreized. First there was the darkness of Puritanism, then the sickness of Victorianism, followed by a brief burst into the sunlight in the Twenties and Thirties. Then War Two, when clothing became revoltingly utilitarian and sensible; clothing *qua* clothing (if you call those broad-shouldered female styles sensible; trying to look like the men they were replacing in industry, I suppose). After that women's apparel was designed by un-men (and some un-women, too!) who hated women, and certainly much of it wasn't designed to decorate. The Sixties brought clothing-as-adornment, as natural to the TV Generation as rebellion and experiments with pot and LSD and sex, because with TV you just can't lie much to kids anymore.

What Kro Kodres had worn depicted his culture, and an Earthly sociologist could have said a lot about Aros just from that clothing: garishly, barbarically bright, male plumage, designed for freedom of movement—a tunic without a sleeve on the sword arm; how clever for a swordsman! —and, adornment.

And now I wore the garb of desert dwellers, nomads. Loose robes that reflected the sun and formed a sort of cage about the body, a barrier between it and the heat. Very effective in a dry climate.

I wondered what the Jadiriyah's at-home clothing looked like, or even her traveling clothes. Which reminded me that I could ride back and find out. Her clothes were back there somewhere behind me, with the late Oth and Ard.

I twisted around to look: yes, I could see the rocks,

looking tiny and unimportant now. I shook my head. Unimportant! They were mighty important to Jadir-iyah-Liz, and to me, too. I had killed. I would never be the same again. I'm not. I have killed. Not at a distance, with high-powered rifles or bombs or grenades or ridiculous distances with heavy artillery. I had killed up close, and swords are personal. Very personal, I remembered, thinking of Oth's wide eyes on me and what I'd done to the right one. I shuddered, and my stomach lurched.

Then the feeling went away. It hasn't come back. I was over the hump. I was a killer. Of men—and saying that the Vardors aren't really men makes little difference.

And I hadn't wanted to go to Vietnam!

Yeah well, I told myself, this was different; it was kill or be killed.

Like hell, inner me snapped back. *They weren't threatening you!*

Yeah, but I saved that girl from slavery or death.

Uh-huh; that's what old L.B.J. said about Vietnam. The Other Side wanted to kill 'em or enslave 'em.

"Yeah," I said aloud, "well, I can *prove* it!" And thus smugly victorious over myself, over Hank$_2$, I got up and ate some Vardor rations and drank some Vardor rations and, in my Vardor clothing, I climbed aboard my Vardor beast of burden and set off across Vardor domain.

To the victor go the spoils!

I rode all day, due west—I hoped—and stopped when the sun was crouching like a fat orange goblin atop the long range of hills to the (?) west (?). (It was. Yes, Aros travels in the same direction about its sun as Earth does. Why not? I suppose the odds are fifty-fifty, I don't know, and as it turned out that isn't germane to Aros anyhow. Aros has very little to do with physics; its existence, I mean.

(Besides, if this message DOES get to Earth, you will certainly never be able to contact me and correct my errors, anyhow! I admit you'd get better explanations, and longer ones, too, if I were science writer Poul Fredrikssen, say. But I'm not, and he probably doesn't do things like grabbing girls in labs and getting knocked on his tail into "Temporal Dissociators.")

I had brought along Kro Kodres' knapsack—my former waterbag and ring-bearer—and I propped it up twenty or thirty yards off. Then, for an hour, I practiced with the short Vardor bows. We will not discuss the first nine arrows. The next two I sank into the bag, the next three elsewhere, and the final three into the bag. Seven others were within a foot of it or had passed no more than a foot above it.

In the morning I spent about an hour plodding about on and off my slook, collecting arrows.

The slook is an apparently happy beast. He does not moan and groan all day like the Earth-side camel (*el-jeml:* "supercilious-head," did you know that?). Nor does he sleep standing up as Earthly horses do. Nor does he swell his gut to fake you out when you're tightening the girth-strap, a favorite trick of horses, who are entirely too clever.

A slook seems able to go on forever with little effort. He can store up enough water and food to operate for days. His walk is less comfortable, really, than his dead run: those long pushing legs in back jar one quite a bit at a walk. But when he flattens out and runs in long soaring leaps the ride is quite comfortable and the landings smooth and not unpleasant

—except for the final one. His braking system is admittedly over-efficient.

It is typically human, typically American, to personalize everything, and I named my riding-slook ERB. I pronounced it as a word, rather than a jammed-together collection of initials, but I think of it as in all capitals. The other animal, plodding along behind us with the gear, I named Kline, which seemed appropriate enough.

We were approaching something green. We kept approaching it for two days. I wondered why I was not seeing any animals and other creatures, and shortly thereafter I did. Birds in various sizes and nonstartling hues, snakes of unstartling size and color, insects and lizards. The green line I was approaching became a forest, and as ERB and I drew closer and closer it sprouted legs: treetrunks of only two shades, either gray-black or red-brown, like mahogany.

I didn't know if it was a jungle or forest, and I wondered why Kro Kodres hadn't mentioned it. I had a choice: either try to bust through or parallel it awhile, in hopes of seeing a road. I had no doubt there'd be one.

Why search for a way through this greenery, why seek out Brynda?

Why not? I had so far met four Arone natives. I didn't belong here. I had no place to go. My one contact was a dead man named Kro Kodres. He was from a place called Brynda, and I had things of his to prove I knew him—unless some idiot decided I had killed him and would be stupid enough to come straight to his hometown. He had apparently been on his way back to deliver a very important message, a message he held back from me, evidently, until he was 101% certain of me—or dying. I wasn't even sure I HAD the message. I merely carried along in my head the words he'd shouted as he died.

I had marked it down in my brain. He'd had no written message. As to the girl: well, her thoughts had given me a clue or two there. She didn't appear to have been his willing companion. As to his having the ring: from what I now knew, I felt he'd taken it from her to put the quietus on her magical powers (I felt silly thinking that, but what else was there to think?). Where they'd been, what they were to each other—these I didn't know. But I could find the Jadiriyah in Brynda, and I would try again. Carefully. Tangling with witches really didn't seem too cool!

I knew nothing else to do. I had been jerked off Earth and set adrift on this planet, as if God, as I had previously suspected, was not dead at all but was quite, quite mad. This way I had a goal: Brynda. I had a name to use, and I even knew someone in Brynda.

I had no guarantee, and the thought crossed my mind many times and still does, that I wouldn't be jerked suddenly up from here and redeposited. Back on Earth, perhaps, in that same lab with Evelyn Shay glaring at me—or in the Atlantic Ocean. Or on another planet, perhaps, where there were critturs called *tharks* and *thoats* and a city called Helium, or where there were *vooklangan* and men living high in monster trees, and Mephis and Muso.

I chewed on that. (I have to; I'm built that way. I can't just *accept*, like a standard brainlessly brawny hero. Besides, I wasn't brawny then, anyhow.)

Maybe . . . maybe Burroughs' novels, and those amazingly similar ones of Otis A. Kline's, and others that seemed pieces of cloth loomed the same day— maybe they ARE true. Maybe there was or is a John

Carter somewhere, a Carson Napier, a Miles Cabot, or that new Cabot, Tarl. Not on Mars or Venus. But somewhere else, as I am. (I should say as I *was,* since I am recording my thinking *at that time,* now long ago.)

Perhaps I'd find others here from Earth, some of those thousands of famous disappearances that have puzzled our planet for centuries. Maybe that famous story about the gentleman—in England, wasn't it?—who walked around his carriage one night and vanished—maybe it's the story of a man who lived and died on Aros, or Andor (which certainly DOES exist), or someplace else.

Maybe Burroughs and Kline and those other writers got the facts bollixed. Or maybe they deliberately placed their stories on planets in the system of the sun Sol, in Earth's celestial backyard, to make their stories—homier. Mars and Venus, after all, are the worlds next door. Aros—well, I don't know. I looked up that day, and I shook my head. I didn't remember that either of the Centaurii was *orange!*

My stolid mount and I plodded along, a hundred feet or so out from where the forest dribbled out to become this perdurable plain—why? Why the suddenness: desert, bang, forest, just like that? It didn't seem possible. The line of demarcation was minuscule. Dust and rocks here, a tiny twilight zone of scraggly grass, and: rich greenery and foliage. I didn't have an explantation, but again I chewed on it, because I *like* explanations. I'd asked why all my life, and I saw no reason to stop just because I was someplace other than Earth.

The dense jungles of Africa and the Sahara Desert are on the same continent, yes. And in California there are floods, snows, vineyards, earthquakes, and deserts. And what else, along with the desert: the world's champion trees! And Aros is certainly bigger than California, or America either. The curvature would be much more pronounced, the horizon a lot closer, the day a lot shorter, otherwise.

But that wouldn't do it. I couldn't sell myself. Deserts don't just become jungles like that—snap!

Things are not what they seem, Hank.

Yeah, well, look Hank$_2$, that ain't no explanation. This world seems more and more the product of a diseased mind!

ERB and Kline and I had by now worked out a pretty decent sleeping arrangement. They seemed able to sleep forever or for a short time, until awakened, and without moving more than a little. For the past several nights I had curled close to ERB, sleeping on his saddle blanket with my removed *stoba* (read "burnūs;" burnous, if you don't know any better) serving as coverlet. We slept that way that first night of paralleling the jungle or forest. It was somewhat warmer at night, although seemingly a bit cooler by day. More impossibiltiy.

Our sleep was disturbed. ERB woke me; I lurched up to a sitting position to see a pair of yellow eyes glowing at us out of the darkness. ERB growled. The eyes blinked. I called. There was no answer. I fitted an arrow to my bow and tried to aim between and just below the eyes. But I had not replaced the cover that had slid off as I sat up. I shivered just as I loosed my long Vardor shaft, and neither roar nor scream of pain greeted my shot. The eyes, however, left, apparently having got the message.

One thing I had noticed: ERB had, for the first time, growled. He WAS closer to the lupine or canine family than to the equine one then, even though his phytophagous nature was obvious: the way he stripped those trees of their leaves!

I took a long time going back to sleep. ERB dropped off instantly.

In the morning I went out to examine the tracks. There were lots: man-tracks. Barefooted. My arrow was imbedded in the ground just in front of the foremost of one set. I must have fair wiped his nose for him. A man, emerging from the jungle to stare at me, in silence. But—a man with *glowing yellow eyes?*

I retrieved the arrow and went back to make breakfast. I led the slooks over to the jungle and tethered them where they could make their own salad.

Using my sword, I chopped firewood from a fallen tree. God bless the Vardors: their flint-and-steel worked beautifully, and the meat from their supply tasted a lot better cooked. I ate, sitting on the thin growth of grass that trickled out from the forest, as if it were trying to fight off the desert—or being driven back by it. I wondered if there were animals in that forest. And what about the spy I'd shot at last night? Big golden eyes that left man-tracks?

They looked like bird eyes, or cat eyes. I glanced at the silent forest. (Why no bird noises?) A cat? *Just what I need,* I thought: *a lion or something.* Very deadly and, as I remember, also fast. I've seen lions only on TV, in movies, and in the Cincinnati Zoo. Mangy looking beasts, like overgrown housecats who still haven't grown into their too-loose skin.

I ate my dried-meat breakfast, wondering about the possibility of edible fruits over in those trees—*and* lions, tigers, boa constrictors, etc. etc. etc. My eating was not so exuberant as the way my slooks went after those fresh tree leaves, snaffling them up with enough noise for sixteen animals.

I finished breakfast, got things together and packed, stamped my fire out—dead out, Smokey—and mounted up.

"Dammit ERB," I told my mount, and he put back one ear, "I'm lonely! Not that you aren't a good ole buddy-pal, but I'd sure like to *exchange* remarks with somebody."

ERB plodded unconcernedly and silently on. But of course I had my opportunity to converse mighty soon. Remember the man-tracks and the golden eyes? Well—

7

Conversation
with a parrot

They wore longish white garments that flapped about
their shins, ridiculously, anachronistically resembling
lab smocks. With boots. And belts, and broad swords
like machetes. They were all dark men, none bearded,
none with as much as a mustache. But with straight
black hair to the shoulders.

Each man had a bird on his head. Yeah, that's
what I said: a bird on his head. A large, green, yoke-
footed, yellow-faced bird with a downcurved beak
that gave him a severe, disapproving expression. And
pop eyes. Parrots. One rode the head of each man—
each attacker. They came swarming out of the jungle,
deployed intelligently to surround me, and halted.
They had blowguns.

I got the message: I lowered my bow and let the arrow slide to the ground.

"Do you surrender?"

A raucous voice, an ear-tearing, head-knifing voice:
a parrot's harsh voice. I looked at him. He looked like
all the rest. They appeared to be ordinary *Psittacidae*,
Amazon brand, all of them looking just like Dr.
Blakey's foul fowl, Pope Borgia.

"You spoke?"

"Of course I spoke, man. You think it was one of
these human yoyos? Here: speak for the stranger,
Jummy!" He flapped his shiny green wings, buffeting
the long-haired head of the man he rode. The fellow
lowered his blowgun from his lips and opened his
mouth and spoke:

"Jummy wants a cracker?"

Before I could begin to assimilate that, me and my weak knees and spinning head—much less react with more than a dropped jaw—he added:

"E equals em-see-squared, probably, but who the hell can prove it?"

He spoke in English. Accent: Dr. Blakey's. And I'd heard Blakey say that more than once; he'd taught it to Pope Borgia.

Staring, I managed to firm my lips and most of the rest of my facial muscles. I lifted my chin.

"Great," I said, in English, with asperity. "Is he your —pet?"

Sure it sounded ridiculous. It is a ridiculous concept. But it was there in my mind, and I knew the answer before the green monstrosity replied:

"What else? I asked if you surrender?"

I looked around. I was surrounded by blowguns, most of them leveled at me. I nodded. "Kamerad. I mean—I surrender. You don't speak German too, do you?" I decided against adding "ugly." One should be careful about insulting one's future—master.

"Blakey, you and Hank take charge of those beasts of his. Mishay, bring his weapons. All right you, come along with us."

I couldn't take it seriously. It wasn't possible. The men said nothing—except Jummy, when prompted, as one prompts a pet or a child to do its thing. (No, I don't equate them—you do. Did you have your child do *its* thing today, for Gramma or Uncle Charlie or Mr. Roberts?) But I looked around, and what I saw was a circle of Amazon headhunters complete with blowguns—and lab smocks. I tried to ignore the latter. It was the former made me nod.

"OK. Where we going?"

"To the Master. Come along."

I went along. Some of the parrot-ridden zombies preceded me, others followed. We went into the jungle. That's what it was, a jungle, not a forest. I've never seen a South American jungle, only movies. But I had the feeling that if I could see an Amazon basin jungle, it would look like this. Trees, vines, undergrowth, extravagant flowers, funny noises, all of it. No—not quite. I saw no snakes, I saw no beasts, and every tree was heavy with fruit, most of it hyper ripe; the clichéd word, I think, is "lush." I didn't see a single fruit that wasn't ready to eat— yesterday. Perfect parrot food.

So we went through that jungle, and we didn't see any snakes or jaguars or even guinea pigs. I felt as if I were on a Hollywood set, like those false-front Western towns. I felt as if I were maybe a little crazy —or more than a little. I wanted to sit down, I wanted to go to sleep, I wanted to go someplace and have a long solo skull session.

I had an unsane thought as to who/what I was going to face, and of course I was right. The silent men with the green birds surmounting their stringy-haired heads took me to their leader, their Master, and he and I stared at each other.

"Hi, Pope Borgia."

"Oh shit! It's that damned Hank!"

"Pope Borgia, on this planet you may be a bigheaded big-ike, with a bunch of parrots riding on your human pets. But I'm not one of them. I'm an alien to Aros as much as you are. For all I know we're the only people from Earth here."

He regarded me from his round, staring eyes, his head cocked. He blinked (or nictitated, whatever the phrase is for yellow-faced, green parrots).

"You calling me a people, Hank?"

"Pope Borgia, it is obvious to me that you are a people. You are in charge here, and you and I are conversing. I don't know *how*, but we are. Sure, I'm calling you people. And I'll tell you this: I'm really glad to see you."

Another long, silent scrutiny: popeyed. "Hank, you make me want to cry," Dr. Blakey's lovely parrot said. "Really. But I can't. I watched Evelyn, and I tried, but I can't do it. I'll tell *you* this: I'm glad to see you, too. You call me people. Hank, I'll be oxidized if I don't make you an official parrot, I swear I will."

"Well I'll be oxidized"—a favorite Dr. Blakey expression.

"I'll be honored," I said. "And I am now going to sit down."

I did. It wasn't my idea; my legs just didn't feel like standing up any more. There I stood, on a planet called Aros, in an Amazonian jungle, surrounded by Amazonian headhunters—in lab smocks —with blowguns in their hands and parrots on their heads, telling them what to do. I was conversing with a parrot who could converse. A perfectly normal Earthside parrot who (that?—he's a "who" to me!) the last time I had seen him had possessed a vocabulary (constantly extolled by his owner) of forty-seven words. That is if you count "E equals em-see-squared" as five, which I'd felt was cheating a little.

And I had called him a people, and meant it, and he had promised to make me an official parrot, and I had said I was honored, and I meant that, too.

It was too much. I sat.

"This is my friend," Pope Borgia said. "His name is Hank Ardor, he is from my hometown, and he's an OK guy. As a matter of fact, regardless of appearances: he is a parrot. Treat him as such."

Every parrot nodded. Every parrot-topped head
nodded.

I was accepted.

I was a parrot.

"Did he send you too?" Pope Borgia asked later, as
we messed about, sampling assorted fruits. He had
given me a little something he'd found and brought
here with him: Dr. Blakey's chiming watch. Reversed. It must have been mighty heavy for a parrot
to carry while flying. He'd gripped the chain.

"No," I said. "I, uh, it was an accident."

"Swell. Where d'you think we are, Hank?"

"Pope, I haven't the faintest. It's called Aros. It's
another world, another sun, different moon—moons.
You understand *planet?*"

"Sure." He raised one wing a little, which I took
for a shrug. "I understand about all of it."

"Can you account for that?"

"Beg pardon?"

I sprawled on the grass at the base of an enormous
black-trunked tree. It wasn't a banana tree, but
that's what it bore. Bananas. "Pope, I don't want to
insult you or anything like that, but let's face it: parrots are bright birds. They can imitate human speech,
even words. Some of them can be taught to repeat
simple sentences, especially cockatoos and—"

Pope Borgia made an ugly noise and I stopped and
started again. I'd already asked him how come no
cockatoos or macaws or toucans, all members of the
parrot family. He had advised me quite positively
that green is a beautiful color and he hated showoffs
in fancy clothes.

"—Amazon parrots, the lovely green ones," I finished with a trace of dissembling, and he preened.

You realize that I use that verb literally, for once. "But—there's never been a *conversing* parrot. I mean, you're thinking, and we're talking just like two—people, back on Earth."

"Sure."

"Well, let's face it, Pope, you couldn't do that back on Earth. How come you can here?"

He stared at me out of those big round eyes. "Never thought about it. Dr. Blakey and pigeon-chest —Evelyn, I mean—"

"—I recognize the description—"

"—popped me into that bell thing of his. Suddenly I was very sick and in darkness. Then I was outside, in the bright sunshine. All I could see was a lot of yellow ground and some mountains. I don't like mountains. I don't like dust. I started flying. I didn't know where I was going. But I flew—what else was there to do?"

"Nothing at all," I replied; after all, he'd done precisely what I'd done, save that he came by air.

"Right. So after awhile I began to worry about all that yellow ground and no trees and everything. I thought how nice it was to be free. But what I wanted was a nice jungle. Just like home, with plenty of fruits and more parrots. Well, I kept thinking about it. And I kept flying—on and on. All of a sudden here was the jungle: home. Only better: none of those nasty snakes and stupid, noisy monkeys. No jaguars and things.

"It was all just what I wanted. I mean, me in charge. Humans as pets. Everybody talking to everybody but the humans just staying shut up till they're told to speak or asked a question. They aren't too bright. We take care of them. They make good pets. They can clean up after themselves, too."

"They look just like the headhunters you must've seen in the jungles back home," I said.

"Yes they do. It was a gang of guys just like these that captured me. About twenty years ago or so. That's how I wound up in America. Blakey bought me in a pet shop. He worked alone for years, you know. Talked to me all the time, teaching me to talk. I heard everything he said. After awhile I was understanding most of it. But I couldn't seem to *say* all of it. I always thought how nice it would be if I could talk, you know, conversation. Just like people. But I couldn't seem to do it—until I got here."

"Maybe this is a dream," I said. "Maybe we're dreaming? Hm, maybe we're both having *your* dream."

Pope Borgia looked about at the surrounding, goody-laden trees.

"Blakey used to talk about parallel worlds. Parallel universes. Said there was an infinite number of possibilities. It seemed likely to him that every possibility was a reality, somewhere. What the hell's 'infinite,' Hank?"

"Too many and too much to think about. It's a phrase people invented. We don't understand it any more than you do; it means endless. Anyhow . . . you think—" YOU THINK! I paused to ponder that a moment. Yes, he sure did. Pope Borgia *thought*. "You think that this is one of those infinitely possible worlds, huh?"

He bobbed his head. "Sure. What else? This is the world where parrots run the show and humans are dummies. Except you, of course."

"Well, that would explain some of the odd stuff— like those parrots of yours, and their pets, speaking English," I said, thinking, frowning at an enormous yellow fruit swaying in a little breeze. "But—it leaves some holes." I told him about Kro Kodres, and Jadiriyah, and the Vardors, and slooks. He listened, staring popeyed at me.

"Wow. Weird. Us parrots talk parrot talk and English. Our pets talk English, period. Give us some Kro Kodres talk."

I did; he didn't understand it. "Damn! I'm out of it again! Another lousy human language to learn—excuse me, Hank. So what's your theory? *I* wouldn't be dreaming any of the stuff you've been talking about. You?"

"Hm." I watched the yellow fruit, swaying, swaying. I glanced at big-eyed Pope Borgia, perched on a low limb, looking hunched-up, his head cocked on one side, staring at me, waiting for the Word. I finally shook my head, fingering the backward-faced pocket watch.

"Maybe . . . but uh-uh. I wouldn't have dreamed about a gal who didn't bother to thank me and left me stranded on the desert. That's not wish-fulfillment, that's for sure!" I am a firm believer in Freudian dream interpretation. "Besides, I'd have dreamed her looking like Sophia Loren, not Elizabeth Taylor."

Pope Borgia wagged hs head. "Pigeon-chests, both of them." He puffed his chest. "You should've been born a bird, Hank. ALL of us are chesty! But her name was . . . what?"

"Cor Jadiriyah."

"What's that mean?"

I frowned. It wasn't a name, of course, I knew that. That's why Kro Kodres had always put the "*cor*" in front of it: "the Jadiriyah." A title, obviously. But I hadn't tried to work out a meaning. What does "colonel" mean, or "janitor"? Besides, I'd had entirely too many mindblowing things to think about, and I'd just set that one aside. Now Pope Borgia prompted me to dope out what I should have done long ago.

Jadirn is a ring, in this language.

Riyah? Iyah? Nothing.

But wait—this was a pretty young language, pretty simple. Not overdeveloped and synchretistic, like English, from lifting pieces and patches from a dozen and more other tongues. Here words still retain their original meanings. "Reeyek," then (spelled r-i-y-e-k). It means "to wear, to put on." I nodded slowly.

"I'll bet jadiriyah means ring-wearer," I mused aloud. "And it's a title. From what I saw, it must mean 'sorceress.' Evidently she didn't have the power to vanish, without the ring. With it—poof! So . . . a ring-wearer is a sorceress. A ring-wearer, *the* ring-wearer, the jadiriyah. Sure!"

"Maybe," Pope Borgia suggested, "her name's Elizabeth Taylor."

I looked at him. He'd goosed me to dope out ring-wearer; now he gave me another thought. A tenuous wraith of a thought that drifted about the corridors of my mind like a tendril of fog—or maybe a tendril of light, *in* the fog.

"Oh god, Pope Borgia, I hope not! It's all insane enough and mixed up as it is. But—oh lord!"

8.
The jungle
that disappeared

I couldn't stay there in that nutty Parrot's Paradise, and Pope Borgia, who admitted his subjects were a bunch of dummies anyhow, elected to accompany me. ERB was a little nervous, but didn't seem to mind overmuch the garrulous, sharp-voiced bird who now rode my shoulder or saddle-horn or flew about us. But before I take this account away from Pope Borgia's jungle kingdom, there are a couple of things I want to mention.

First, the men: they weren't. They were, as he had put it, real dummies. Without the parrots I swear they'd have stood around or collapsed and eventually died of starvation or thirst. They not only didn't have the sense to come in out of the rain, they wouldn't know rain from an apple or a banana from a banyan tree.

Second, another theory: that this place was not a dream, but a dream-phantasy. Certainly it was, in Pope Borgia's case. But not in mine. Would I have postulated what I'd been through? Well, maybe, but not that snotty Jadiriyah, certainly. I still remembered clearly the conversation Evelyn and I had had that night, about Burroughs and the position of women in barbaric cultures. Sure, a sorceress would have been accorded respect—or else. But I was just as sure that I'd not have postulated a sorceress. A sorcer*er*, maybe. Probably *me*, which would make me superior here, brawny or not. And certainly I would not have wished up a scene in which I drained helplessly out on the sands, while a beautiful woman, less than a mile away, was being ravished. Surely my own concept would have been that I'd got there in time, downed the baddies just as I had, and availed myself of their erstwhile prey—who would have thrown herself at me. THAT'S a male dream-phantasy.

Which left me nowhere. Aros was a somewhere world, with a lovely paradise for an Amazon parrot named Pope Borgia, but with a series of blows and paradoxes to damp the spirit, blow the mind, and quell the ardor of Hank Ardor. It seemed a planet designed to blast the theories of Aristotle and Ayn Rand. If A, then A is—sometimes. Contradictions do not exist, except—when they do. Contraries may or may not be. Black is black, but it might also be white, tomorrow, or this afternoon, or when the sun goes down, or if someone rubs a magic ring. If this is so and this is so, then this is so—maybe. Yet it wasn't so pronounced that I would call it a null—A world.

Things just weren't what they seemed, and they weren't necessarily so, either.

There was another possibility, and I liked it less than any other:

This was some sort of experiment. Capitalize: Experiment. I was in a lab, along with (according to his official papers) Rodrigo de Lancol y Borja, The Lord Alexander Pater Patrum VI: Pope Borgia. We were performing beneath a giant microscope, and someone, some gigantic scientist or god, was noting down our reactions to a series of oddities.

As an experiment, I had the distinct impression that we were not working out.

And the final possibility, at least the final one I could then conceive: we were Controlled. We were puppets, bestringed marionettes, performing at the behest and in accord with the plan of some Secret

Master or Masters. Worse: we were performing at the
behest of some planless Secret Master who was quite
insane.

I'd have been better off of course, just to have gone
along, to have accepted. But as I have pointed out I
am not built that way. I kept asking why.

An hour or so after we rode away from the purlieu
of His Holiness the Borgia Pope Alexander VI, I had
another of those shocks, and another *why* to add to
my mental list.

I glanced back. No reason, I just did. We were
riding along, paralleling the jungle, plodding forward
toward the roadway I was sure must eventually cut
through it to put me back on course to Brynda.

"I wonder what we're going to find?" Pope Borgia
said.

"People," I said. "A city. Lots of people, normal,
non-parrot-ridden people. A way through the jungle.
Maybe even a caravan."

"What's a caravan, Hank?"

And for some reason, thinking about the possibility
of a caravan, which reminded me of the possibility
of Vardors or other hostiles, I twisted around and
looked back.

Behind us lay only the yellow desert. Beside us
and ahead of us the jungle lay, and it ran back a little
way behind, and got sort of misty, as if it were an
out-of-focus film. And then a few yards back it just
stopped.

But we had been riding along beside it for at least
an hour!

"Oh god!"

"What is it, Hank?" Pope Borgia turned to look
at me, saw me looking back, and twisted his head
to follow my gaze.

And there was the jungle, a long line of green running back as far as I could see. I blinked and touched my forehead; I felt weak, not for the first time on Aros.

"Huh? What is it?"

I shook my head. "Nothing," I said. "I think I'm getting too much heat." And I rearranged my cowl-type headdress. I stared ahead, squinting. Watching a long dune-hill grow and grow as we neared it.

"What's a caravan?" Pope Borgia asked again; I had forgot he'd asked.

I told him. A long line of people, probably on slooks, with some slooks loaded with packs and maybe a carriage or three or sedan chairs mounted on slookback or something like that.

"Oh," he said. And, tensing myself, biting my lip, gripping the reins as if they were likely to flicker out of existence even as I held them, I looked back.

Desert. The jungle was gone again. *Oh, god!* This time I just kept quiet about it. It wasn't happening. It couldn't be happening. I was going over the edge. I'd been too long in the sun, I'd had too much sun-glare blasted up into my eyes from the bright saffron dust, I'd been too long without human companionship. I jerked my head around.

"Why don't I do something about this suspense," Pope Borgia said. "I think I'll just fly up ahead and see what's on the other side of that hill."

"Dune," I said, rather mechanically.

"Pedant," he snapped, and he took off with a lot of flapping. Then he sort of soared on ahead, moving swiftly forward with lazy-looking flaps of his ragged green wings.

"Bighead," I muttered, in Arone: *Sorrfelinas.*

ERB (and Kline, I guess; he just plodded along behind us, content to follow in the footsteps of the head slook) and I watched as Bighead/Pope Borgia flapped on, climbed, turned, went sliding down and out of sight beyond the dune, then popped back into sight again. Returning. People or not, he was still a parrot, and he couldn't seem to help imitating a stoned rock combo while he flew. But *he* didn't like noisy monkeys!

He braked above my head, slid sideways, and came down on my outstretched arm—protected with a strip of leather cut from Oth's belt; I wore Ard's—with a great backflapping of wings. ERB shied and snorted, even going so far as to growl, once. He cranked his neck around to peer back. I patted his neck: "O.K., big boy," I told him, and he believed me and turned his head and kept on plodding.

"See anything?"

"Caravan," Pope Borgia said.

"Really? Oh wonderful—what's it look like?"

"Lots of colors. A long line of people on slooks. A lot of other slooks with packs on them. Three have some kind of funny little houses on their backs. With curtains. I couldn't see in. Some bigmouthed creature swiped at me with his goad. Another tried to put an arrow through me! I think we'd better get into the jungle, where it's safer."

I glanced over; the jungle was there. I wasn't about to look back. Why feed one's psychotic delusions?

"We'll be O.K.," I said. "All they have to do is see you're with me."

"What if they don't like you?"

"Uh—" Suddenly I realized that was a possibility. Purely aside from standard barbarian-type xenophobia, I was nattily begirt in Vardor desert garb.

"What were they wearing?" I asked.

"All sorts of stuff," Pope Bighead said, with that wing-shrug of his. "Mostly like what you're wearing. But other things, too. In lots of colors—all light. White cloaks."

I sighed. We'd be all right, then. I wouldn't be pounced upon as the foremost of a contingent of Vardors, anyhow. All I had to worry about was xenophobia. Well, I thought, think positive. *They're gonna love you. They'll welcome you with open arms.*

A rider appeared on the dune: a burnūsed, slookmounted man in a white cloak. He shaded his eyes, looking at me. I wagged my arm. After a time he waved back. He wheeled and vanished behind the dune. By the time I was half-way up its long slope, he was back. Again he halted, looked, and again I waved. He paced his mount slowly forward, and he had company: two other mounted men, both in white cloaks, both with ready bows. I had already pushed back my hood to let them see I wasn't blue-gray of skin, and I kept my hands in plain view.

They came in on both sides of me, slowly.

"Who are you?"

"Name's Hank Ardor," I said. "Who are you?"

"We're three and you're one; we'll ask the questions."

"We're *two!*" the parrot snapped. "Are you blind?"

The man goggled. "That bird talked?"

"No," I said, "I'm a—sure he talked." There wasn't any word for "ventriloquist" in my vocabulary, and that was snotty anyhow. "His name is Borgia."

"A strange man wearing Vardor clothes and a bird that talks—and both of you with funny names." The man glanced at his bow-bearing companions, then shook his head. "Where are you from?" His eyes were on the chiming watch. I'd supplemented the chain with leather and hung it around my neck. It ran. Backwards.

"Earth," I said.

"I haven't heard of that one, either. Where the Dark Power is Earth?" (Dark Power; Power of Darkness: *Falkh.*)

I swung an arm. "Miles," I said. "Beyond the mountains on the other side of the desert. Where are you from?"

"Brynda. But there isn't anything on the other side of the desert. Besides, how could a lone man cross it anyhow?"

I grinned. "It wasn't easy," I said. I slapped my chest. "The Vardors didn't *give* me this clothing. And the bird was a lot of help. But—Brynda! I met a Bryndoy out there, this side of the mountains. Vardors had put an arrow in his belly, and he had a broken leg. He'd dragged himself into a cave. They'd taken his slook and I guess couldn't be bothered making sure he was dead—he was dying, and couldn't have got anywhere without a mount. His name was Kro Kodres."

The man looked at the others. "You know that name?"

One of them nodded. "Of course. He's a Guildsman —I mean was. Little fellow, beardless and slender?"

I grinned at him. "Uh-uh. Scalplock, short beard, thin mustache. Built big; huge legs and arms. He also had a ring, which he asked me to deliver to a lady he'd left. I did, incidentally killing two Vardors who'd got to her first."

"A ring! Who was she? Where is she?"

I shook my head. "Brynda, I guess. A lot of gratitude she showed me, for the ring and for saving her from the Vardors, too. She grabbed the ring, slipped it on, and—" I decided to run a test—"you know what happened then."

"She vanished."

"Right. I don't even know her name; she didn't stay

long enough to tell me. She's the jadiriyah of Brynda.
Hair so black it's bluish, big dark eyes, spoiled-look-
ing mouth, very thin, straight nose—big in the chest
and short in the leg."

Their eyes were big, all three of them. "No wonder
she didn't stop to pass the time with you! That was
Sorah!"

"Oh." Sorah? So what? "Who's she?"

This time all three of them laughed. "You're telling
the truth, fellow, and you're certainly not from this
part of the country! She's the daughter of Guildchief
Shahara of Brynda! But surely even she offered Julan?"

"She did. So what? I wasn't after a reward."

They exchanged a look. "How did she act?"

"Disturbed, grateful, sort of. Then she took the
ring and vanished. She didn't bother to say thanks, or
offer to bring me along."

The man who'd known Kro Kodres laughed.
"No, I'm sure she didn't." He looked at the first man.
"He tells the truth about Kro Kodres, and certainly
about the Shayharan Jadiriyah, Stro Fentris. I—"

"How do we know he didn't slay Kro Kodres?" the
other bowman asked. His partner looked at him as if
he should have a parrot on his head.

"Why would he kill a Bryndoy, then ride toward
Brynda and tell us he was with Kro Kodres when he
died, slook? Hank Ardor doesn't look that stupid to
me."

"Thanks."

"Anyhow, Fentris, I'd say we may as well believe
the rest of it. It will be easy enough to check in Brynda—if Her Bitchiness will deign to identify him. And
another man wouldn't hurt us, at all."

Stro Fentris looked at me. "You're a warrior?"

I shrugged. "I managed to put away a couple of

Vardors," I said, wondering what he'd say if I showed him a few of my mind-boggling calisthenics.

"Why are you heading for Brynda?"

"Kodres gave me a message to deliver. Apparently it's important. It's verbal, not written. And I am interested in seeing that beautiful jadiriyah of yours again, if I can find employment in Brynda." I wondered what skills I had. I'd had enough of the adventurous life to have no further desire for secretarying.

He nodded. He was a broad man, full-bearded beneath his cowl, which was white—and lined with black, like Kro Kodres' cloak. "I will not ask you the message," he said. "Who is to receive it?"

"Uh—I don't think I should tell you that, either," I said, hoping that would be acceptable. I had no idea who was to receive Kro Kodres' cryptic words. The Jadiriyah, I supposed: Shayhara Sorah.

"All right. We are about to enter the jungle. Will you put your slook in the caravan and accompany us?"

"Will you give me a receipt for my pack slook?"

He laughed. "I will give you a receipt, Hank Ardor, and I think we are well-met."

"I hope so," I said, and I went back over the dune with them and down to their caravan. It was within thirty feet of the jungle, which was pierced by a broad cleared lane of grass. Some of it was rather high, but jungles have always been reluctant to allow any permanent encroachments. Stro Fentris introduced me to the caravan master—Fentris was commander of the Protectors—and I watched them insert Kline into the line of slooks.

The next day they were given the opportunity to decide for themselves if we were well-met or not, and if I was or wasn't a warrior.

9.
Sophia Loren
and Dejah Thoris

I wasn't a captive, I wasn't a guest, and I didn't really belong. I was a foreigner, and worse, a foreigner from someplace they'd never heard of. I had the appearance of a warrior and I told a story to go with the appearance, which would be easy enough to check in Brynda. I wasn't exactly accepted, but I wasn't rejected or shunned either. I was reminded of Western movies. This guy or group of guys meets another guy or group out on the plains somewhere. All are armed: every man a castle. The groups or individuals join, or camp together, friendly but not overly so, nor loquacious, and wary. The newcomer(s) may be OK and he may not. *We'll let him join us, sort of, but he has yet to prove himself.* This was the way I felt the Bryndoys looked upon me.

It beat being taken prisoner, or press-ganged, though, and I wasn't too uncomfortable.

The caravan had decided to camp here at the edge of the jungle; it would set out early in the morning and be out of the trees by the end of the day. The men I'd joined stayed apart from the others, aloof. They were Guildsmen, Protectors: professional warriors employed as escort. Their leader was Protector Chief Stro Fentris. While the caravan had a Master, Fentris did not take orders from him. The Master would, I learned, take orders from Fentris in the event of trouble. Which seemed to indicate a caste system, with warriors on top. I wondered about a priesthood, hovering above them all like vultures, collecting money by officiating at births, namings, weddings, funerals. And reading auguries, probably.

Aware of my position and the American Western analogy I'd mentally drawn, I didn't ask much in the way of questions. There were no priests with the caravan, at any rate.

As we ate—the Guildsmen having reversed their cloaks to the dark sides, as I'd anticipated—Stro Fentris asked me a little about my trans-desert, trans-mountain "country": Earth. I told him we had a ruler and a senate of old men, controlled by businessmen and the military. He nodded.

"It was nearly so in Brynda, once, before my birth. Warriors and merchants were so far down the scale they contemplated forming some sort of government in which everybody shared. Then came the wars, and the Vardors, and warriors gained power. A bright chief named Kro Fars realized what power he and his warriors had, how valuable they were. He set out the idea of the Warriors' Guild. It formed slowly, and flourished—mostly after Kro Fars was assassinated. The last real struggle was fifty years ago, between the priesthood and the warriors." He grinned, displaying big strong teeth, the left incisor minus a wedge-shaped piece. He had a scar on his cheek, too. "The Guild won."

I shook my head, testing their wine: it was good. Not too dry, but not horrible thick stuff like port, either.

"Warriors defeated priests in a power struggle? How could that ever be done?" It sounded like a dream. I'd always cherished such a notion: doers conquering parasites and taking over! At the time I left America/Earth—well, skip it. You don't need

me to tell you that those of us who worked and paid
taxes were slaves to those who didn't. I imagine America has had its revolution by now. Have you re-in-
stituted capitalism yet?

Stro Fentris of Brynda was grinning again—lord
that man has big teeth!

"It wasn't hard, as it turned out. The situation was
ready to fulminate when Itza attacked Brynda. The
army of course was ready, at government orders. But
the real fighting men were the Guildsmen, and the
Guildchief called a strike. The situation grew warmer
and warmer. Then, when the Itzoys were almost at
the gates, the government capitulated and took
away the power of the priests. The Guildsmen went
out and smashed the Itzoys and then kept on going,
to take and sack Itza. Once you defeat an enemy's
army, it's stupid not to cripple him at home, too!
The Guild was the hero—and the Guildchief was
smart enough so that it took a very short time for the
people to be convinced that the Guild WAS the hero,
first last and always, and that it was the fault of the
priests that Brynda had almost been taken by Itza.
The Faith had made conditions so miserable for the
Guild that its members just couldn't generate en-
thusiasm to fight for such a structure."

He shrugged, still grinning, and swiped about in
his tin plate with the last biscuit, sopping up every
droplet of gravy and juices.

"The priesthood never recovered. And now there's
a temple to Kro Fars."

Which didn't sound much better to me; clobber
one religion, one pyramid-topper, in favor of another.
Then turn it into a religion because people *like* smoking opium. Apparently the Guildchief was top man in
Brynda, and the warriors were the top of the heap—

which is why they swaggered, and ate apart from the rest of the caravan. The elite.

The Guildchief—Shayharan. With a daughter named Sorah. A ring-wearer or sorceress. Whose life I had saved. Hell, I *had* rescued the princess!

But—she hadn't even bothered to say "Gee, thanks."

Our caravan had been to Itza and points east—notably Rizadar and Risathade. The Protectors' presence was required because of:

Vardors;

Itza ("one never knows about Itzoys!");

assorted bandits, outlaws, etc. etc. etc.;

Saghritar. One never knew about Saghritoys, either. Mainly because of religion, they'd been the enemies of Brynda and Itza and Risathade for a couple of hundred years.

I looked around. "There seem mighty few Guildsmen along, Chief," I said, "considering all those possible dangers." I wondered about parrot heads.

Stro Fentris nodded with a grim expression. "Nineteen," he said. "And five of them Itzoys, at that. We've lost twenty-six men since this ill-omened caravan left Brynda three months ago. Fourteen of those are recovering—hopefully—from wounds in Risathade and Itza. The others have retired. One of them, for Fars' sake, was retired in a tavern brawl in Itza!" He shook his head. "Three Vardor attacks, two duels, that brawl, and those thieving renegades between Itza and Risathade!" He glanced around, and his chest came out: "But the caravan's intact."

Retired, I thought. Of course; when have fighting men ever said "died"? It's always been "bought it" and "K.I.A." and suchlike. I wondered if smalltown newspaper editors printed death notices saying that so-and-so had been "called," or had "passed over," and so on. No, of course not. There are few small towns on Aros. And no newspapers. There are men here who make their living with pens, naturally, but no publishers' pens in any community—or country either.

Stro Fentris was regarding me—as merchandise.

"I hope we're through with trouble," he said. "It's been a terrible journey for the Guild. I wasn't Chief when we left Brynda, and I'd rather have got the job in some other way. But if anything else *does* happen, I hope men know how to fight, where you come from."

"They do," I said, "although a lot of people wish they could forget."

Which was approximately when the Vardors attacked. I say approximately; I can't be sure, of course. Someone yelled, and then someone else, and then hooves were pounding and thoughts buzzing about like a dozen disturbed hives, and an arrow seemed to materialize about a foot from me, quivering in the ground.

"BOWS!" Fentris bawled, bounding up and away from the firelight. An excellent idea. I jumped in the opposite direction. And forgot to compensate, so that I wound up ten or more feet away. Probably nobody noticed, that time. "COVER!" Fentris was shouting, and he rattled off four or five names: "—the litters!"

I had barely glimpsed the contents of those litters: one man, two women, one of them with a child. All were overadequately swathed in desert clothing. Now it was night, partially moonlit night, and as I looked I could see the three litters, removed from the backs of their slooks. They were set about a smallish fire like three points of a triangle.

And Vardors were streaming in from the desert on two sides, on slooks, and out of the jungle on a third side, afoot. I may have had a choice (run, wait, or charge), but it lasted only a moment. A slook came barreling in at me, and his rider was screech-roaring and swinging his long sword.

I moved. The leap put me so far out of his way that he galloped on past, without even trying to rein after me. He was now after one of the Guildsmen Fentris had detailed to rush to the litters. The man was loping to his post on foot with bow in one hand and quiver in the other. The mounted Vardor plunged after him.

And I pounced after the Vardor. Leap number one carried me some thirteen feet forward. While I landed, jackknifing and launching myself again, he covered some ten feet. I took off again, and let out a yell to try to attract his attention. He was still howling, and the Bryndoy warrior had spun about to try to meet the charge: pretty hopeless, unless he got lucky with an arrow into the behemoth galloping upon him. My leap number four landed me on the Vardor's slook behind his rider. Before I fell off I drove my sword into the gray man's back. The blade went deep; the slook galloped on; I fell off. The sword hilt was dragged out of my hand.

Falling isn't too bad for me, here. I don't exactly float, but I do come down pretty slowly. I let myself crumple, and as I rolled in the dust I saw the Vardor going sideways out of his saddle, wearing my sword hilt between his shoulder blades. The slook headed out for the desert. I rolled. As I came over again I saw the man whose life I had probably saved. He was running over to the Vardor. By the time I got up, muttering and groaning a bit, he was by my side, extending a bloody sword: mine.

"My life is yours, Hank Ardor," he said, and added
his name: "Thro Alnaris."

"Keep it. Return the favor sometime. Thanks for
the sword."

We grinned at each other with a brief flashing of
teeth. Then he took off again toward the three shadow-
shapes of the litters. I expect the child was screaming,
and maybe the women too; I couldn't hear them, in
the din. Nor could I be sure how much of the awful
clamor I heard was inside and how much outside my
head. In times of stress these people broadcast something awful, as if the adrenalin shoves the thoughts
out piecemeal and at maximum volume. And I know
now, of course, that I am probably the finest receiving
set on Aros.

I wanted to go someplace and bury my head; I
didn't. I was hyper-adrenalized too, and there was
blood on my sword and I felt like superman. I had
overtaken a galloping slook, bounced onto his back
and slain his rider, and saved a warrior's life, by his
own admission. I glanced around, gripping that
bloody sword, for another warm body in need of
cooling.

There were plenty. There was the smell of slook
and leather and blood, the sound of battle cries,
screams and howls of pain, shouted threats and commands. Moonlight glinted on metal and shiny leather and firelight flickered eerily from the faces and
churning legs of running, fighting men. A slook
screamed as it died, rolling so that its Vardor rider
sprayed blood from his crushed body. A few feet
away from me the kid who'd brought us fresh fruit
from the jungle sat on the ground with his face pale
as the moon. He had both hands clamped around the
arrow in his middle, and he was staring at it as if he
just couldn't believe such a thing could be growing

out of him. Beside him lay a bloody Guildsman. Another knelt by the body, sending arrow after arrow into the night; I'm not sure if he had specific targets or not.

Two Vardors were coming for him on the run, from the jungle, both of them with bared swords, one of them holding up the skirts of his robes as he ran. I yelled and bounced.

The archer looked up. He started to swing his nocked arrow at me, then twisted his neck to follow the direction of my pointing sword. Immediately he swung about and sent off a shaft, which went between the two attackers. A minor miracle, that; they were almost touching each other as they ran. His hand went back for another arrow, fitted it and drew it in one beautiful motion. It passed me as I rushed past him. With my agility I saw no reason to wait for the attack; I might as well attempt to confound the opposition with some calisthenics.

The one who was holding up his robe hem yelled and went down. If he'd left the silly robes to swing around his legs, however binding, the arrow might not have gone through his calf just below the knee. The other one glanced at him, glanced at me, started to turn to flee, and died as both my sword and another Bryndoy arrow sank into him.

One of the litters was burning. In the bright flamelight I saw a Guildsman raise his bow, loose a shaft, then drop the bow. He had sprouted an arrow in his face. He dropped, and as he fell I saw two Vardors falling upon a second Bryndoy warrior. I headed that way.

As I arrived, settling down in a bouncing leap that had carried me over the head of another Vardor, I saw that I again had a choice:

The two Vardors had the Guildsman hemmed. Although he was doing a good job, apparently inventing fencing on the spot in a series of furious clangs of metal on metal, he couldn't survive. Both were two feet or more taller, both had a lot more reach; both had longer swords. That was on my right. On my left:

A big grinning Vardor was dragging, by her hair, a robe-swathed woman out of her burning litter. She was yelling. He was laughing.

A choice, and I didn't hesitate.

Obviously the couple on my left would wait: he may have been giving her a little pain in the hair and face, and perhaps a sore bottom, as he dragged her by her dark mane. But he obviously was not about to kill her. Not at once. The two Vardors on my right, though, were not interested in capturing their Bryndoy opponent; they were bent on carving him to get at the litter behind him. The girl would keep. Raising my sword, I jumped.

I miscalculated. Instead of landing just behind the taller Vardor, I slammed into his back and bounced off. We fell, he forward, I back. I wasn't floating this time, I was rebounding, and it hurt. I grunted and woofed and floundered, trying to hang onto my sword without bloodying myself on it. I looked up to see the other Vardor swinging around. His face split into a big gray grin, the firelight dancing on his teeth and on the sword he swung up to bisect me.

Then his eyes and mouth went wider and he stiffened and the sword came down very slowly and he fell forward. I scuttled out of the way, glancing at him as he slammed into the ground beside me. His back was all over blood. I looked up past him.

"Thanks, Thro Alnaris. You return favors fast!"

"I hate being in debt!" he said, grinning, and pivot-

ed on both feet, swinging his red-smeared sword up
and down in the same motion.

Which, with a nasty CHUNKing sound, took care
of the almost-man I'd knocked down. Thro Alnaris
was glancing about for danger before he had his blade
out of the twisting Vardor. I got up, fast, nodded at
Alnaris and at the litter he'd made his responsibility,
and looked at the other litter. It was about gone. The
flames had shot twenty or thirty feet up, swiftly con-
suming the lacquer on the wood and the silk or
whatever the curtains were made of. Now it had settled down to chewing away at the palanquin's wood.
I jerked my head around in a half-circle.

My eyes picked up the Vardor just as he slung his
female bundle across a slook and thrust a booted foot
into the stirrup. As he swung his other leg over, I
started running. One, two, three, four, then five running steps, and I jumped. It was probably my longest
jump so far; maybe twenty feet. As before, I came
down rather slowly, having time to feel my innards
floating around in the prolonged freefall. Then I alit,
doubling my legs until my tail was close to the ground.
And I launched myself again.

The Vardor wheeled his slook. Perfect: that way I
came flying into him broadside. Both of us went off
the other side of the beast, which snarled, rolling its
eyes, and reared. The woman slid off his withers
to plop to the ground a few feet away from me and
my new opponent. We were wallowing, each of us
trying to grab and hack at the other.

Now I learned a lesson. On Aros I am one hell of
a jumper. With that jump I had saved a life or three
and dispatched several of the slate-fleshed attackers.
On the other hand I had never been any fair shakes
as a wrestler; I'm not built for it and had never

tried anyhow. This time I was in way over my head: I was trying to wrestle a 300-pound, eight-foot opponent with arms like a gorilla's and strength to match.

Both our swords dropped. He just let go of his, and when he started squeezing me, over my arms, mine slipped out of my hand. He started to put on the pressure, grunting. I started dying. The night got blacker. The noises began to fade. My tongue lunged out, trying to find some way to curl around some air and drag it in. There was no way. I don't remember my last thoughts.

He grunted again, louder than before, and I made an uglier noise as he suddenly exerted more pressure. But then he was heavy against me, the pressure slackening, and I forced his arms away with my own and sucked in the sweetest breath I'd tasted since the day I'd graduated from college. I looked up past his big head.

I didn't see her face. She had her hood up. But as I looked up at her, the girl he'd been carrying yanked his dagger out of his back where she'd stuck it. She jammed it in again. He grunted again and jerked. I shoved him off and came out from under him.

I repeated the words Thro Alnaris had said to me: "My life is yours."

Her voice, from the darkness of the hood, sounded young enough: "Oh no. You saved me. My life is yours."

I retrieved my sword, taking deep breaths as I did. "Let's don't argue about it," I said. "There wasn't anyone else in that litter, was there?"

She shook her head, turning to look at the last crackling remnants of her palanquin. The flames were no more than a foot or two tall, now, dancing about in delight at having eaten the litter so handily and so quickly, without interruption.

She turned back to me. "You're the man who joined the caravan this afternoon?"

I nodded. "Hank Ardor. Who—"

"You aren't a Guildsman?"

"No, I'm a foreigner. Who—"

"You aren't in the employ of Stro Fentris?"

"No. I was heading for Brynda, and happened to get here at the same time the caravan did." I gave up trying to ask who she was.

"I am glad you did," she said.

I looked around. Just as I turned my head a screeching maniac came swooping and fluttering down and landed on my shoulder, incidentally batting my face half a dozen times with his wings.

"Watch those damned claws, Bighead!"

"Sorry, Hank," the parrot said. "Say, this was a wild scene. They're running now, though."

I was almost afraid to ask. "Who?"

"The bad guys, naturally. What's that in all the robes?"

I looked at her; she was lifting her hands to her cowl. She pushed it back and stared just past my face with enormous eyes. She was staring at the parrot, of course, and I stared at her. Her almond eyes were too big, and too long; her nose too straight, and too long; her mouth too wide, the lower lips too full, her cheekbones too pronounced. A collection of overdone features. Put them all together and they were breathtakingly female; startlingly beautiful.

It was Sophia Loren's face.

"The—the bird talks?"

"What'd she say?" the bird demanded.

"She asked if you could talk."

"Certainly. What's she think I am, anyhow?"

"My familiar, probably. She's looking at us as if we're a male witch—warlock, isn't that it?" I smiled at her and switched from the English the parrot understood: "Yes, he talks, and I understand, and he understands me. He doesn't know your language yet —our language. He's a very friendly bird, too. Name's Pope Borgia—I call him Bighead."

She nodded, the eyes still very big. Lord, but it was weird to be standing there looking at Sophia Loren! Wearing a wig of course, and with a lot of tan; all these people are dark and black-haired.

"Kharik, Sorrvelinas," she said.

"What'd she say?"

"She said 'Hi, Bighead,'" I told him.

He wiggled, ruffling his wings. "Did you have to tell her that name?"

"Sorry," I said, trying to smile at the girl at the same time. I was aware of our rudeness, talking in a language she couldn't understand. "I also said 'Pope Borgia,' but of course those words aren't familiar to her."

"Hmp! Who's she?"

I raised a hand to Bighead's back, stroking the green feathers and hoping he wasn't carrying psittacosis. "He says hello to you too, beautiful lady, and asks what your name is?"

"Oh—I'm sorry," the girl said. "I am Dejah Thoris."

We had killed a lot of them, but they had, too. The water-boy died, and four Guildsmen, and a slook driver and two others. They had also destroyed a litter and slain two slooks and driven off another one, laden with fine cloth about which its owner hadn't ceased moaning by the time we reached Brynda. We counted thirteen Vardor bodies and two Vardor slooks. One of the latter and two of the former weren't quite corpses when found, but that was quickly remedied. I also watched Chief Stro Fentris, with agony in his eyes, dispatch one of his men who'd lost an arm and too much blood and had an arrow sticking out of his groin. He himself requested his euthanasia-by-sword.

I was sitting on the ground near one of the litters, while Pope Borgia shot off his mouth and the girl helped the other woman silence her caterwauling infant. The kid was about eight months old. He had been born in Itza two weeks after his father's death, and his mother was returning him to her family in Brynda. I was mostly sitting on the ground, staring at it and thinking.

First Elizabeth Taylor.

And now Sophia Loren. Bearing the name of, in case you haven't read Burroughs and have forgotten Evelyn's and my discussion back at the beginning of this narrative, the Martian wife of Burroughs' hero John Carter, Dejah Thoris, daughter of Tordos Mors,

King, as I recall, of Helium. A "deathless beauty"—
which is just how I've always felt about Sophia Loren.

I turned it all over and over in my mind, that and
the parrot and his parrot-headed men and the vanishing jungle and a few other things. I couldn't make
it tie nicely together into a package with a card reading "Sense."

I wasn't sure I *was* the protagonist. Come to think,
I'm still not.

I looked up as a pair of boots halted before me.
Then another pair. And another.

"Thro Alnaris says you saved his life," Stro Fentris
said.

"He returned the favor about five minutes later," I
said.

"After he had rescued me again," Thro Alnaris said.

"Thro also says you rescued the girl Thorisan Dejah."

I gazed up at him. "Um. As a matter of fact she
killed the Vardor. And Alnaris slew both the ones he
says I 'rescued' him from."

"And Pro Sharais says you saved his life, also."

I looked from Stro Fentris to the man beside him. Oh
yes, the archer. I shrugged. "Guilty. There were two;
we killed one apiece." *And listen to me,* I thought.
*Talking about killing as if it were something I've
been doing every day of my life and twice on Sun-
days. How come I don't feel sick to my stomach?* (I
did feel a little queasy, but it wasn't urgent.)

"You saved three people's lives and killed three
Vardors, although at least two others should be credit-
ed to you."

"All right," I said. "You three look like judge and
jury, Chief. I admit guilty to all charges."

Stro Fentris shook his head. He put out his weapon

hand—there was blood on the wrist. "Don't call me
Chief," he said. "Stro."

I got up quickly then, and we gripped hands. Sure
it's an Earthside custom. Undoubtedly stemming
from the "Look: no weapons" days, then giving way
to "Look, you hold my weapon hand and I'll hold
yours," when man got shrewder. It had developed the
same way here. It's natural enough, in an arms-bear-
ing society. It still means more on Aros, of course;
the threat is still there. In a few centuries it will be a
formality here, too.

His giving me his name was more an honor. He
was Chief Protector of the caravan. Everyone called
him Chief save his own men; the brotherhood of
warriors all call each other by name, although usually nicknames or surnames, since there are so few giv-
en names in use. (At the time of Julius Caesar there
was only eight first names in use among the Romans.
And "Julius" was Julius' *last* name; his wife and close
friends called him Gaius. Probably half the population of the Republic had that same popular first name.
Marcus, by the way, was a last name, too.)

At any rate, Fentris was accepting me into the
club, telling me to call him what his men called him.
I accepted his hand, squeezed it, gave him a surprise
by pumping it a little, and said, "Honored. Hank."

He nodded. "Hahnk."

And then it was "Thro" and "Hank," and then the
archer: he introduced himself as "Proby," which is
an elongated diminutive for Pro in the same way
Johnny is for John.

We stood there and beamed at each other.

Proby nodded past me, at the two women. "Julan," he said, and all three of them laughed, Thro
Alnaris rolling his eyes. Then they looked at each

other again and we all shook hands again and they
walked off. I turned to the two women and the now-
silent child. Dejah Thoris introduced me to the other
woman. Oh; she too had given me a less formal name,
though not a strictly buddy-pal one. Casual acquain-
tances would call her Thorisan Dejah: "Thoris' daughter—" Strange; there wasn't any word like "dejah"
in my vocabulary. (There still isn't. Her father says
her mother made it up, and her mother is dead.
Sorry.)

"Julansee," Dejah Thoris-with-the-face-of-Sophia
said.

I smiled and bowed my head. "Thank you. I am
honored and delighted I saved you." (Julansee: I offer Reward, or Compensation. A formula, of course,
although I wasn't fully aware of its meaning at the
time. And if you think these people are full of rituals
and formulas, think about yourself. Handshaking.
Waving. "Hello" every time on the telephone, even if
you just saw the caller thirty seconds before. "Dear"
in a letter, even if it's to someone you hate, or to a
magazine. "Thanks" and "you're welcome" and "I'm
in your debt" and all that stuff; kissing and so on. All
cultures are full of formulas. True, they mean a bit
more on Aros; it's a younger culture, and the original
reasons for the formulas and the rituals are still only
a little in the past. New ones are still being born, too).

"Will you be all right with—" I'd forgot the baby's
mother's name already. She and Dejah looked at each
other and frowned, and I was embarrassed at having
forgot and particularly at not having done a better
job of covering it up. Slowly, they both nodded. The
mother looked a little stricken; I couldn't read Dejah's
face.

"I will be close by," I said. "All the way to Brynda."

"Good!" the mother said. Oh, her name was Kronah

something. Feminine of the popular "Kro." She smiled; bad teeth. "Please do, Hank Ardor. We want you to, don't we, Dejah?"

"Of course. And my life is yours."

"Well, since he was busy squeezing me to death and *you* saved *me* by using his own dagger on him, let's call it even."

Kronah's eyebrows rose. "Oh! Is THAT it!"

I looked at her, wondering, then nodded. "I'm afraid it is. I was man enough to knock that Vardor off his slook, but not to wrestle with him! I'm sorry— I will admit I remember Kronah but not your—"

"Don't bother. Call me Kronah," she said, smiling brightly.

I nodded. "Kronah, Dejah Thoris, I think I should go and help the others."

Uncomfortable, wishing a guy could save a life and have his own saved now and then without all the froo-fraw, I turned and left them. Kronah was smiling, just as if she didn't have yellowed front teeth. Dejah Thoris was not. *Well,* I thought, *the daughter of Tordos Mors can't afford to be too friendly to a common warrior—and a furriner at that. Still, it would've been nice if she'd said something, instead of letting what's-her-name do all the talking. And she might've said "thanks," too!*

I joined the other men in time to learn what they did with the corpses of slain enemies, or at any rate slain Vardors:

First they separated them from their weapons and clothing, so that they'd enter the Midworld naked and defenseless, without anything to identify them as warriors. Next they separated them from their heads and crushed the skulls, so that when the bodies entered Midworld they'd be blind and voiceless to identify themselves or narrate their deeds. Third they bound the heels of those headless bodies with ropes and tied the ropes to slooks and dragged them a long way out into the desert. When the slooks were well away, the crushed heads were hurled into the jungle, a lovely business. This so the bodies would have no hope of finding their heads.

They treat the bodies of their own dead rather better, insuring they are without nothing during their journey to Midworld, their stay there, and their ultimate return as infants. Only fools, after all, bother to do nice things for defeated enemies. They might come back again, so that, say, a war to end all wars might repeat itself a short time later.

When all the stripping and butchering and dragging off and throwing into the jungle was at an end, Stro Fentris and Thro Alnaris came to me, carrying a collection of robes and weapons. Those of the two Vardors I'd slain, plus those of the two who'd had Thro hemmed against the litter. I agreed to split with him, after a brief friendly argument. We discarded most of the bloody clothes, but it occurred to me that the weapons and belts and so on would represent currency = food in Brynda. Proby and I worked out the same arrangement with the two we'd slain together. By the time I had it all sorted out and secured together, Kline had a pretty hefty pack. Or would have; Kline was one of the slooks the attackers had killed. They'd probably vented their anger on him when they saw he was laden with Vardor gear. I sighed. And the Vardors hadn't left behind any mounts, either, not live ones. I suppose the ones whose masters were dead either followed the others: herd instinct, or were mindcalled by the fleeing "men."

One can't have everything.

In the morning we wended into the lane through

the jungle, with the parrot I now called Bighead answering the cries of other birds in the trees. He disappeared several times, once for hours. I didn't question him. Everyone always yaks about the birds and the bees. But my dad told me about people and dogs and the like, and I STILL don't know how birds Do It. Or bees either, come to think. There aren't any bees on Aros. I hate honey.

The causeway through the jungle was wide enough for about six slooks abreast; we rode with two abreast, for the most part. It was very cool, quite dark, and blessedly un-dusty. I learned that Dejah Thoris was carrying a great deal of money, mainly in the form of the "checks" used between the three friendly cities. She had snatched it and thus saved it when her litter was burned by a Vardor arrow. The short, slender merchant in the third litter was not at all happy to be turned out, but both the caravan-master and Stro Fentris insisted, and the fellow sullenly bestrode a slook while Dejah Thoris remained invisible in the palanquin. It was pretty much that, rather than a slookback howdah. While at present both she and Kronah rode in their curtained little houses on slooks, the litters were designed for hand-carrying; only the carrying-poles need be slipped through their rings.

The litters were separated by five pack slooks and two Guildsmen between. I rode beside Dejah's. Her curtains remained closed, but I saw her twice that day, and we exchanged some words and pleasant smiles. Something seemed a little funny, but she didn't put on the childish act with which the original Dejah Thoris had tormented that Carter fellow.

When we stopped for lunch and again for supper and to camp (a little past sunset; we were determined to get out of the jungle) I remained with the protectors. I had assumed the jungle would yield onto a savannah or rolling farmlands with horizonal hills, and I was not disappointed. A rippling savannah stretched out and out to give way to obvious farmlands dotted with trees and occasional animals in the distance. Farther still, a series of gentle hills nudged the sky.

"May I ask questions?" Stro Fentris asked, as we finished eating.

I shrugged. "May I neglect to answer some of them?"

He laughed. "You came from nowhere. You talk to that bird, who talks to you—both of you in a language I've never heard. You are not a Guildsman, or even of Brynda, but you fought as well as any man."

Huh, I thought. *Better!*

"And now you remain with us, rather than with Thorisan Dejah. Also you cannot mindspeak. And there's the matter of your agility."

"A man needs some talent to compensate for a closed mind," I said. "I receive thoughts very well, though."

"I noticed. I believe you receive thoughts better than anyone I know—unless there's another explanation for your 'hearing' me and coming this afternoon; you should have been out of range, as it turned out."

"I'm not with Thorisan Dejah," I said, "because that widow has her eye on me, and they're together every time we stop. Naturally enough; they're the only two women along. As to my receiving thoughts—" I shrugged. "I've no explanation."

"Um. How far can you leap?"

"Pretty far. You saw?"

"No, I didn't. But I've had enough men tell me. What's that gold disc you wear about your neck?"

I glanced down at it: Dr. Blakey's chiming pocket watch. Since the chiming bothered me, I had pushed the stem to hush the thing up. Why did I wind it? —habit, what else? It's a watch. One winds watches, whether they mean anything or not.

"Something that belonged to someone I liked," I said, which was truthful enough, if evasive.

"Are there jadiriyahs where you come from, Hank?"

I shook my head. "Your countrywoman is the first jadiriyah I've ever met," I said. "Or heard of."

"Hm. And you—are you a sorcerer?"

I thought about that. Sort of, I thought, on Aros. I could talk with a bird—with, not to. If Stro was right, I was a better receiving set for mindspeak than he and his people. And certainly I could jump a lot farther and higher!

"Sort of," I admitted, thinking that it might help me but surely could not harm me.

"I thought so," he said. "What powers do you have?"

"Uh, remember I didn't promise to answer every-thing? I will pass that one. I'll admit I can't mind-travel myself, like your Bryndoy jadiriyah, though."

"What will you do in Brynda?"

"Stro, I don't know. Maybe I can find someone to recommend me to the Guildchief."

We exchanged smiles. And went to sleep, and trav-eled for two more days, uneventfully, and came at last to Brynda at the foot of Bryno Mountain.

It was one more in the series of shocks that were beginning to make less and less impression upon me; shock was becoming commonplace. The thing about Brynda was that it was exactly what I expected to see. As a matter of fact if you'd like to have a precise picture of it, look it up; I'm sure I've seen it in an old

Alex Raymond *Flash Gordon*. Sky-aspiring Brynda is an exact replica of that picture, mostly in blues and whites and pale yellows and tan and pale gray.

Add that to the list.

11

The man who
was not Tordos Mors

In Brynda, Kronah made certain I knew where she'd be, and extended an invitation. Dejah Thoris seemed to disappear. The caravan-master and Chief Fentris took me to the rich—and of course grossly fat—man who'd financed the caravan. He made wheezing noises of delight, gave me a reward of ten silver pieces —squared coins with off-center holes, for stringing on breakproof gut and hanging on one's belt, safer than a purse. He offered me a job. Fentris advised him I was a foreigner, not a member of the Guild, and the fat man apologized—to Fentris. He told me to come back and see him if I should become a Guildsman. Then he apologized to Fentris again.

This damned Guild, I thought, *has a real stranglehold on Brynda! That man's obviously rich; he should own the Guildchief and the Guild as well!*

We walked through the busy—and startlingly clean—streets to Guild headquarters. I commented on the streets; Fentris shrugged.

"No slooks allowed in the city," he said, "and no wheeled vehicles. One walks or has oneself carried. It's a lot safer and avoids a lot of noise and filth."

I smiled at the pissoirs: little stalls here and there along the streets, where a man could step in and relieve himself. Superlatively convenient and—momentarily—private. Except that one could both see the feet and hear the stream splashing into the basin. And, occasionally, one could also smell the basins.

But I now understood the city's double walls, and the many stables, both private and for rent, that lay between them. Fentris had got ERB put into the Warriors' Guild stable number three, to save me the price of food and care. Bighead had flown off outside the city, advising loudly that he'd have no trouble finding me. I sniffed, but was unable to detect the distinctive aroma he'd mentioned.

The desk soldier at Warriors' Guild, Protector's Division scowled and stared while Fentris introduced me and detailed my prowess.

"This man is both a foreigner and a scab," the man said.

Fentris stood taller and jutted his chin. "This man has saved three Bryndoy lives, two of them Guildsmen. He has a warrior's prowess, the price of admission and dues, and I sponsor him. Fill out the forms."

The fellow did, churlishly, while I watched grinning. True, I hadn't been in what America for some reason calls "Service" with a capital S. But I knew that this officer who wielded a sharp pen had many and many a counterpart on Earth, most of them just as snotty. But with more authority. On Aros fighting still comes first, and the sword is a damned sight mightier than the pen. Sex isn't obscene here and neither is war, and the system of legal duels holds down the insult quotient.

I signed the document with a flourish and reluctantly counted out the price of admission and first semiannual dues: ten pieces of silver. The fat caravan sponsor could have sent it over and saved wear and tear on the coins.

Walking out, I asked Fentris about being called a scab.

He shrugged. "Well, he's technically right. You

acted as a protector of the caravan, but you aren't
—weren't—a Guildsman. Under other circumstances
you could be in a lot of trouble."

"No one is allowed to wield weapons but union
members?"

"Other than in self-defense, no. And even then a
man *can* get into trouble. Say a caravan that set out
without Guild protectors. It is assumable that it will
be attacked. If it is, and the civilians successfully de-
fend themselves, both the caravan-master and the
sponsor are in trouble. That isn't self-defense; they
should *know* that a caravan needs proper protection.
Now if a man's home is broken into and he slays or
drives off the thief, that's another matter. But if it's
his place of business . . ." Fentris shook his head.
"Obviously such requires Guild protection and should
have had it."

"Damn!" I took time out to ogle a passing woman
wearing a loose gown to the ankles—slit on the left to
the hip. Fentris, by the way, now wore just what
Kro Kodres had worn: the one-sleeved red tunic, too
short, over matching trunks, and the reversible
black/white cloak. Also a brass-studded leather cap.
He had not been Chief when the caravan left Brynda,
and had not appropriated the rank marks of the man
whose place he took after his death. Thus Fentris
wore no rank marks at all. I wore some stuff he had
persuaded (without much difficulty) the caravan-
master to give me: a white tunic, two-armed and knee-
length, a broad yellow sash, and a short, purely dec-
orative cloak of something lightweight and green. I
wore Kro Kodres' arms and boots, still too big. Yes,
I had a callus on each foot, and another coming on the
left.

"What would—well, say the caravan we just brought

in had not had any of you, and had been attacked, and we'd managed to beat off that attack the other night. What would happen?"

Fentris nodded; I followed his gaze to the woman bending over to inspect the fruits on a wandering merchant's cart. We grinned and paused to watch until she straightened. She raised an eyebrow at my companion before wriggling away. Uniforms get women, every time.

"Such a case is hardly worth considering," Stro said, "since the caravan would never have returned. But, IF it happened that way, you would be arrested and prosecuted as a scab. The caravan-master and his sponsor would be Listed—and pay heavy fines."

"To—"

"—the Guild, of course."

"Ah." On Earth, States support themselves by stealing money from convicted lawbreakers in lieu of punishment. On Aros, at least in Brynda, the Guild enriches itself the same way. Plus collecting its fees from members. Plus taking a sort of agent's commission for arranging the protectors for an expedition such as the one just completed. Plus collecting the insurance premiums. And since the Guild also sold the insurance, I wondered just what form of pressure might be used in selling short- or long-term policies. Capone called it "Protection," didn't he?

The Guild, I quickly learned, was also good to its own.

Stro and I entered the main Guild Headquarters and after thirty or forty minutes were admitted to the office of the Secretary. He eyed me while Fentris explained, nodded, and finally stood to extend his hand. He too looked a little surprised when I shook it rather than merely gripping it. He called in a secretary, sent him after something, and sat back to ask me a few questions. I had expected to meet Guild-chief Shayhara and now realized how silly that was; he was a Big Man, the boss. I wonder how far ahead the warden has to make an appointment to visit Hoffa in his cell?

Which is unkind; the Guild is an honestly-enough run organization, and Shayhara was not a criminal or even a Bad Man. Certainly, he enriched himself; he was the most powerful man in Brynda. (Besides, his daughter was a sorceress.) But I have never found evidence of his using extralegal means. Pressure and power, yes. But if one presumes those to be extralegal one must postulate that the entire House and Senate of the United States is criminal, and then where are you?

The Secretary's secretary returned with the requested papers, which Secretary Parnis studied. At last he looked up.

"Stro, I am recommending that your position as Chief be made official and permanent. You should hear from the Guildchief within a week or so. Meanwhile, I will exert my authority to grant you the right to wear the White Stripe."

Stro nodded with a smile. "Good," he said, without saying thanks. He and I and Parnis all knew that Stro Fentris was qualified to add the white border to his tunic sleeve and hem: Senior Commanding Guilds-man: Commander. Parnis looked at me.

"You are a warrior of note, certainly, from that one encounter with the Vardors. Two Guildsmen and the daughter of Pro Thoris owe you their lives. And now you are a Guildsman First—which Fentris says took the exact amount Fatpockets gave you." He smiled. "Which is why he gave you ten silvers. Anyhow, with

Commander Fentris' permission I am awarding you ten percent of the insurance premium for that caravan. It will house and feed you for a while."

"Justified," Fentris said, and he went over to sign the tablet Parnis pushed at him.

Parnis was smiling, leaning back. "I don't mind telling both of you that if that caravan hadn't got through I would be out a year's pay—I had a few little things sold in Risathade, and they sold well. If the Vardors had got away with that money . . ." He shook his head. "Anyhow, I assure you, Ardoris, that I'm delighted you ran onto the caravan and joined it! Which reminds me. I would suggest we Bryndize your name unless you have objection. It would be less complicated—and wise."

I shrugged. "I don't mind 'Ardoris,' " I said, "but I'm mighty attached to my first name."

"Just put the legally-required preface on it, Parnis," Fentris said. "Kro Hank Ardoris should be satisfactory. If it isn't—we can worry about it later."

Parnis nodded, called the secretary back, dictated, filled out some stuff, and gave me a chit with his signature at the bottom and WARRIORS GUILD: *Office of the Secretary* at the top, followed by my (new) name. It was a letter of credit, representing ten percent of the insurance premium paid by the individuals and groups involved in the caravan—including Kro Parnis, I guess. I refuse to go into amounts and a discussion of Arone money, but I will say that the premium was fairly high for one three-month risk. On the other hand, considering the magnitude of that risk and the cost in lives. . . .

"What happens to the rest of that insurance money?" I asked Stro as we left the big new building.

"It goes to the widows of the Guildsmen killed in the operation."

"And if they weren't married?"

He shrugged. "More for the widows. Why pay an old man with a lifetime behind him for the death of his son, who chose to enter the Guild of his own accord? It's the widows need the money, not the old."

"Um. Are you married, Stro?"

"Three children."

"And you've been ushering me around rather than going home to play with your children . . . 's mother! Thanks, Stro, but stop it and go home! Parnis said Dejah's father is Pro Thoris, on the Street of Artisans. Where's that?"

Stro shook his head. "First go back to the WGPD building and draw a uniform," he said. "Hang onto those papers from Parnis. Ask them there where the street of Artisans is. A man doesn't go about the city in *clothes* when he can wear a Guildsman's uniform!"

"Oh, yes—say, am I likely to be assigned to night watchman duty over some wine shop, or something?"

Fentris nodded: he was silently pointing out a succulent young woman again. This one had two children in tow, but hadn't lost her figure in the process of birthing and feeding them; she looked equipped to nurse quintuplets. We took time out to watch. Then he answered: "No, Hank, not if I have anything to say about it. And I have."

"You don't want to stop over at WGPD with me for your white stripe?"

He laughed. "Hank, I've had the stripes ready for my wife to sew on for two years. I'll be handing them to her ten hugs after I get home."

Which was a charming way for a married man to measure time, no matter how much standard street-ogling he did. We shook hands, I was invited to dinner, and we parted. I returned to the Warriors' Guild: Protectors Division building to draw my uni-

form. An hour or so later, decked out in eye-dazzling
scarlet and the black-and-white cloak, I was following overdone directions to the Street of Artisans. I
swear the man gave me the same directions three
times, and repeated "You can't miss it" twice.

Naturally I did, and asked directions twice more
—the second time learning that I was *on* the Street of
Artisans, and that that was Pro Thoris' right over
there.

The Arone Dejah Thoris' daddy wasn't king of
Mars or Helium or Aros or top man in Brynda, nor
was he anywhere near top man in Brynda. Perhaps
he was king of the silversmiths; he was mighty
good. But that's what he was, that big man who
looked far more like a warrior than a delicate-handed
artisan, a shaper of silver into statuary of any form requested or conceived in his mind. He had some gut,
naturally enough, because he was a big man, but he
was not what can be called fat, unless you're strictly
Pepsi generation.

His hair and beard were interesting. The hair was
jet black of course, and crispy wavy, without dressing.
On a line above the approximate center of his bushy
eyebrows he was bald, from front to back, his head
looking like a black-grassed yard whose owner managed to cut one swath before his mower broke down.
On either side of that shiny brown bald stripe his hair
was jet black—to the ears. Below that, without any
twilight zone of gray, it was white. His mustache was
black; his beard black with a central white stripe
roughly imitating the bald swath on his head. Later
I learned that he had the same white stripe in the
curling black hair of his chest.

He had the height of Ron Eli with the thick shoulders and arms of Rod Steiger, and those hairy hands

looked like anything but a delicate craftsman's—but have you ever seen a dentist that didn't have big hairy fingers? His eyes were the liquid brown you'd call "melting"; very warm and friendly. He wore a leather smock over his knee-length brown tunic, and he was barefoot. Pro Thoris wore footgear only when he had to, and he or Dejah or his apprentice swept the whole place—shop with studio and living quarters—twice daily. At least. If he stepped on something in his bare feet the whole establishment got swept again, with Pro Thoris groaning and cursing as though he'd crippled himself for life. (After the sweepings the broom straws were carefully, meticulously collected.)

He was alone in the shop, weighing silver when I entered. He looked at me.

"You're the man from the other side of the desert," he said. "I forget the barbarous name. Come in. SKINNY!"

Certain I'd heard a full stop rather than a pause between "come in" and the shouted "Skinny," I didn't act insulted. I was right. Skinny was his apprentice, a young man of maybe twenty (he turned out to be fifteen; these people die younger and mature earlier and look old sooner). He was over six feet tall and weighed maybe one-fifty. He too wore a leather smock—with about five burned places in it and some fascinating stains.

"Take over, Skinny. This is a guest: he saved Thorisan's life." Pro Thoris turned the deep brown eyes on me. "What in Falkh's your name again?"

"Hank Ardor," I said. I'd decided to hell with being Kro Ardoris; thousands of people who'd anglo-saxonized their Polish or Jewish or whatever names in America later wished they hadn't.

"Right," he said, shaking his big head, and he gave me a good grip. "Come on back for some wine, Hahnkahdah."

We passed through the shop and the hanging at the back, then through his jumbled studio, showing me that he believed in juggling more than one project simultaneously, like a writer, and through another hanging into a kitchen. He waved at one of the two chairs at the big table. Chairs and table were beautiful wood, fitted together with grooves and wooden pegs rather than twine or nails.

"Did you make this furniture, Pro Thoris?"

"Of course. You can't buy anything like this without selling your next life—and it would still be sloppily done. Nobody takes any pride in his work anymore, since all this trade started with Itza and Risathade and those other barbarous places. Hm . . . here."

Silver mugs. Beautifully tooled and chased; his work, of course, and I commented on their perfection. Seating himself at the table angled beside me rather than across from me, he smiled.

"Don't gush—save that for my *company* goblets. Going to finish 'em one of these days." By which I learned that I was not being given super-guest treatment, and that the work of art I held in my hands was his "everyday china." I wondered how he'd feel about Melmac. Barbarous.

"I want to get something said to you so we can have it done with, uh . . ."

"Hank Ardor," I supplied. The wine was good, and I poked my snoot in it again to disguise my smile.

He shook his head. "Bar—well. Ahdah? Ahdah. Anyhow, Ahdah—I see it's *Guildsman* Ahdah now, good for you—I want to thank you for saving my daughter from that barbarous beast out there, and tell you that it is impossible to ask more of me than I will give."

It was partially formal; the last phrase was, anyhow. But he meant it. I felt that I could ask for a house-size bust of myself and he'd kill himself or go broke trying to make it. I bobbed my head and handed him my goblet.

"Good," I said. "Lay some more wine on me."

He took the goblet and reached for the pitcher—beautifully hand-tooled silver, of course. "Lay some . . . interesting expression! A bit barbarous, here. You're a bibber?"

"I was drunk once when I was seventeen and I decided not to do it again," I told him, gazing at the nearly clear wine in my mug. "But I like to drink, yes."

"Hm . . . have to let you try some of that barbarous Risathoy stuff some night. Distilled grapes." He shook his head. "Interesting. Slides down like hot butter and then gets up and kicks you right in the head, if you're not careful."

"Brandy," I said. "My people call it brandy."

"Brahndy? I call it slookfoot. Kicks the same. About your people—"

"Beyond the desert and beyond the mountains across the desert," I said. "There lies America."

"You'll be going back?"

I stared into my cup, wondering how sad I really was as I said, "I—don't think so."

"Customs are different over there?"

"Very different, yes."

"Well, they seem to make men pretty much the same way, although—! How're the silversmiths?"

I turned my mug. "Would you believe not this good? You said people don't seem to take pride in

their work—that's the way it is in my country. Everything's done communally, and that destroys personal
pride in creation. Nothing works and nobody cares,"
I added, remembering Ruark's last article.

"Hmph! If that's the case, you'd better have a
look at my company goblets before you leave. They're
almost finished. Started 'em nine years ago. What
about the warriors there? Guilded?"

I shook my head. "Not exactly. Army, controlled by
the government—we think. Conscription, mostly,
and ugly uniforms so that a man can't swagger. And
too many of those who join voluntarily are looking
for a womb. It is that."

"No pride in that. How d'you explain the paradox,
then, Ahdah? You say craftsmen and artisans are
guilded, and take no pride in their work. The warriors aren't, and they don't either. Here the warriors
belong to the Guild—I mean *belong*—but the pride is
unbelievable."

I shrugged, realizing he was a shrewd man; he'd
certainly pierced that one fast! I'd been wondering
about it myself. I decided to worry about it later.
Maybe it was this, or something near: the Guildsmen
were unionized, but *warriors*. While any sort of orga-
nized warring depends by definition upon coopera-
tion among the members of the "team," a sword is
still a mighty personal weapon. You can napalm a
rice-farming village—or your own troops—or blow up
a city or blaze away into the jungle with a high-
powered weapon, killing one or a dozen or dozens.
All without *seeing* the enemy. Glory? Pride? No, just
long-distance impersonal killing, like spraying a
swamp with insecticide to zap the mosquitoes you understand are there, without ever having seen them.

Nice or not, Moses' sixth commandment to his errant people or not, face-to-face fighting depends on skill and strength and nerve and it instills pride. That's in the first place; even though unionized, each man is a single unit when it comes down to the Arone nitty-gritty. In the second, a man can work a lifetime on Earth tightening Screws a, c, and e-1. Without them the car would fall apart as it rolled out of the plant. But—that screw-tightener doesn't know what the hell he's doing. He didn't *make* that car. He's just one of many who touched it, piece at a time, as it went by. And finally: what the hell pride can there be in helping make a machine designed to enter senility precisely thirty-six months—the normal mortgage period—after it is made?

There was more involved in the pride and success of guilded Arone warriors, of course, but I didn't think of it at the time and I am trying not to cheat; trying to tell you things as I learned them.

I told Pro Thoris that fighting was less personal where I came from (he questioned; I mentioned arrows and spears). That even though life was incredibly cheap and there was too damned much of it, people felt constrained to pretend that violence was not an innate trait of man and that life should be preserved—even if it were little more than the kind of stiff, uncommunicative preserves that comes out of jars.

"As to Bryndan industry," I said, wanting to get off the subject, "I wish I had a lot of money. I will have to find a way to make a lot of money. Then I'm going to become your best customer. You are an artist."

"This he tells me after seeing my everyday tableware," the silverman groaned, rolling his eyes. "If you ever have the money to realize that asinine ambition,

I hope you also employ someone with taste to do your choosing." He shook his head and muttered a word. I didn't hear it, but I was sure it was "barbarian."

"Naturally I had to express my gratitude for my daughter's life, Hank Ardor," he said—he didn't pronounce it that way, but I believe I had made it sufficiently implicit how they pronounce my name and indeed all *r*'s, and I see no reason to beat a dead slook. "I want you to know that what I said is true: I am in your debt, and you cannot ask too much of Pro Thoris."

I frowned a little: *But*—I thought. . . .

"But," he said, "we have swords to cross, nevertheless."

I put a "Gee, how's that" look on my face. He didn't mean it literally, of course; Arone figger of speech. We had a crow to pick or a bone to split. Hair? I seem to be forgetting Amerenglish. . . .

"What's wrong with my daughter?" he asked, seeing after a pause of several seconds that I wasn't going to bite.

I cocked my head at him; one picks up the damndest habits from one's friends! "Sir?"

"You heard aright, Ardor. What fault do you find with my daughter Dejah?"

I evoked a mental image of her. Not difficult. What man can't mentally bring up that face and figure whenever he chooses? (And what man wouldn't like to materialize her rather than her image!) What was wrong with her? Nothing! Not to me! Her face: sensual female. Her lips: made for kissing. Her body: sensual female.

I smiled. "Nothing," I said. "Very definitely nothing, Pro Thoris. She is a woman, a very desirable woman. She is Woman."

"She's a silly damned child, but that's beside the

point; she does have her mother's face and form, thank god, rather than mine! In that case I must ask further. Is there something wrong with you? Pardon my asking—but why then did you insult her?"

I chewed on that awhile before I answered, carefully. "Pro Thor—"

"—call me Thoris."

"Thoris, remember that I am a stranger here. I think there must be some custom I don't know about. I assure you I didn't intend to insult your lovely daughter." I grinned, man to man: "You don't think I came here to meet *you*, do you?"

"Hm. No, I don't . . . and you don't look like an art lover either, despite what you say. Did my daughter offer you Julan?"

"Yessir. She said it very clearly: 'Julansee.'"

"And—"

"And . . . well, I thanked her. I told her I was honored, as I remember."

He was leaning forward. "And—"

"And? And? That's all!"

His big fist came down on the tabletop with enough force to make my silver mug jump. I caught it just as it reconnected with the table.

"Exactly! That's all! So she told me, weeping as if her heart were twained, poor girl. How could you possibly have ignored her? It is no more than custom, of course . . . but a man is a man, and made the way he is. It's more than custom makes him accept, unless she is a totally abominable woman!"

I sighed. "Stranger, remember? Obviously Julan means something here that it doesn't mean in America."

He stared at me. "Could your people be such barbarians?"

I rose. "Thoris, I didn't come here to listen to you

call me and my people barbarians, and I'm tired of it.
I'll go out and find a slook and send him in so you
can try to build yourself up by berating him. Falkh!
Have you considered taking up literary criticism?"

His gaze was as open as mine. "Ah, sit down, Ardor.
You know by now I don't really mean it. What I have
I've made; you would not believe my beginnings.
And you know what Frood says about a man's adult
life being affected by his childhood."

Frood? *Frood?* My knees went weak. I'd heard it
before, in just such a context. I'd had a history professor who pronounced "Freud" as it looked, rather
than the usual "Froid." We'd grinned at him, we
superior teenagers in the back of the room, listening
to a lecturer who knew more than our combined
knowledge taped and collated and printed out. But
—Frood? What the hell was Sigmund Freud/
Froid/Frood doing on *Aros?*

I sat. I reached for the pitcher.

We fenced a bit more, and then Pro Thoris explained the custom of Julan to me. Maybe you've already figured it out and feel smugly superior about it.
I've noticed that it's a lot easier to figure out what's
going on when you're reading about it rather than involved in it. That's what enables lit'ry critics to earn
(?—receive) their bread. I knew a fellow once who
read one book about the Africa War in World War
II, and immediately pointed out what a dummy
Montgomery had been. My friend won the whole
business, in a month or so, on paper. I told him drily
it was too bad Montgomery hadn't had him there;
the world would never have paid such tribute to Rom-
mel. My friend did not consider that the situation
might have been a bit more difficult to figure, close-
hand and personally involved.

Anyhow, Julan, and excuse me: my dictating this is

pretty much stream-of-consciousness. I haven't any
written script, of course; I haven't bothered. Julan,
with a lowercase letter, means reward or compensation. Julan, uppercased, refers to the compensation/
reward offered a man by a woman he has saved from
something or other. "Julansee" means "I offer reward," literally. But it isn't the literal translation that's
important or germane; it's the ritual meaning that's
important. In a "barbarian" society (or in any society,
in wartime), the conquerors naturally rape every
woman in sight. Not even the stern old lonely god
of the children of Abraham frowned on that practice!

Conquered—or rescued—women were fair game.
When American soldiers liberated a French girl or
girls from the hands of the raping Nazis, they didn't
sit down and play pattycake with the girls, no matter
what Van Johnson and John Wayne did. Rescue a
lady and she's yours. Maybe for the moment, maybe permanently.

Well, Aros is culturally a little beyond that phase.
The brave warrior doesn't *claim* his reward. The girl
offers it. If she doesn't, he then lays claim, and her.
But she always does. It's custom. They are a sexually
healthy people, and even when the priesthood was in
power prior to the rise of the Guild, the religion was
not antisexual. When the offer is made, a man does
not refuse. In the first place only a genitalless idiot
would, unless the lady involved were absolutely re-
volting. In the second place, a true gentleman, a man
of honor, goes ahead and accepts the offer even of a
creature with a face and bod her mother couldn't love.

So, I had rescued—sort of—the powerful jadiriyah
Solah, daughter of the even more powerful Guildmaster. And she had offered herself, and I had turned
her down. Which explained her odd look and perhaps
her curtness.

Certainly she hadn't *wanted* a sensual session at that point, and I *had* been nice about it, too new and dumb to know what she was offering.

Then I had rescued Thoris' daughter Dejah. She had established first that I was not a hired protector (whose business it is to save lives, and thus who do not merit Julan—unless the lady happens to want it: the connection of danger/pain/sex is well known on Earth). Dejah offered Julan. All she could read into my apparent decline of her offer was a churlish displeasure with her as a woman. Of course the matter was also complicated by the widow. I suppose I gave her more encouragement and hope—nondeliberately.

Maybe I sound pretty egoistic, but I've *told* you: it wasn't a personal thing. It's *custom.* Is it egoistic for you to say your neighbor was hurt because you failed to return his greeting this morning?

"So, Thoris. There it is. I plead guilty by reason of stupidity—ignorance of a custom *my* people would find barbaric."

He nodded, either ignoring or swallowing the turning back on him of his favorite word. "I see. And I will explain. Dejah will be pleased, or at least mollified. You gave her a tremendous blow right in the self-respect.

"As a matter of fact she lost nine pounds while on the journey—but she told me a few minutes ago that she's going to diet. Thinks her body was too lush for your tastes."

I had talked before with fathers about their daughters—but never this way! "You know better than that," I said. "But—"

"Of course I do. And I told her, too!"

"All right, you're her father. Tell me what to do now."

"Get up and get out of here," he said without cogitation. "She will be home in a few minutes; she's out transacting some business for me. Aside from saving her silly head, you also saved the nice profit I turned on this caravan. Go! Get out. I'll tell her; I will explain."

"But—uh—I—" I finally put a check on my stammering and nodding, and I headed for the door. Back through studio and shop, and through the door to the street, dizzy, disappointed.

But as I was leaving he called with humor in his voice: "And come back for dinner!"

I walked stupidly, dazedly down the street, wondering. Was the Julan custom deferable?

12

The answer
that did not satisfy

On the street a half-hour or so later, I met a Guildsman. There were plenty about. I stopped him to ask
about lodgings, explaining who I was and why I was
lost in his city. He accepted it; I was, after all,
wearing the uniform, and the penalty for imperson-
ating a Guildsman was too severe for anyone to dream
of doing it. He directed me to Mama Selapah's, and
Mama Selapah was delighted to see me. She had two
vacant rooms. Since one of them had been permanently vacated due to the demise of its former tenant
in a caravan returned only today, she was happy to
give me my choice. She specialized in renting to
Guildsmen; four others lived in her old house, and
she was careful to lay the word on me that she still
had a vacancy and could sure use the money.

She mentioned something that two others had mentioned: my hair. Naturally the WGPD barber had
given me a Guild scalplock hairdo, but it would be
months before I had that thin mane hanging down
my back. Telling her I was from elsewhere and had
only just joined the Guild, I got her out of my room,
wondering if she had a couple of homely daughters
she was anxious to shove at nice young Guildsmen.
No, probably not. She was just one more kittenish old
landlady, widowed and surviving handily and vi-
cariously by renting rooms to single men.

I stretched out on the bed and stared at the ceiling.
Aros. Monsters (tame ones and otherwise: slooks and

Vardors). Talking parrots—*conversing* parrots. Witches. Julan. Liz Taylor, Sophia Loren, and Dejah Thoris. And me. I knew far too little, still, but here I was in Brynda, a certified scalplock-carrying Guild warrior. With uniform, and sword and even some money: sort of an insurance dividend.

I thought about the stories I'd read. The two from that West Coast publishing company, by Nuetzel: standard gambit. Lowly hero winds up someplace else and gets the princess—after a suitable time of her treating him like dirt. The Burroughs pastiches by Edward Bradbury—too bad his middle initial wasn't "R!" Same bit: first person hero sees upon dropping onto Mars is the friendly neighborhood princess. Odd: she wasn't in danger. But she got that way fast, and he had to rescue her. Terrible problem: the jackass, just like John Carter and Carson Napier and all the others, falls in love at first sight but learns he can't marry her—until the last chapter. And all of those heroes rubbed shoulders with kings and princes and even emperors.

I rubbed shoulders with a mercenary officer and a silversmith. *I* saved a girl—and rather than insulting her by immediately laying sword and self at her feet, I put her down by turning down her "Bed me" offer! There seemed no standard problem between us, otherwise. She wasn't betrothed to any wicked prince somewhere, and she wasn't a few miles up the social scale. Her daddy would explain my ignorance, and I was invited to dinner.

I remembered a conversation Evelyn and I had had back on Earth; it seemed years ago, even then.

"Well," Evelyn had said, talking about her book (which is all anyone who writes wants to talk about anyhow), "first there'll be a universal language. Oh, there'll be dialects, but the language stems from one root, and this planet (she'd named it Afrodyte: Greek goddess plus tokenism) is young, so the language hasn't changed all that much yet. And of course there'll be monsters, and—"

"Are the inhabitants egg-layers—with breasts?"

A withering glance: "No, they're just like we are. But all darker, with black or brown hair and brown eyes, of course; darker races are the vast majority, and this is a very warm planet. They will ride on odd creatures—either dragon-descendants or enormous dogs, I haven't decided."

"How many legs?" I asked, studying hers.

"Oh, six or eight or ten. Certainly nothing standard. After all—"

"Evelyn, four legs seem sufficient. I mean, perfect balance. And for the matter of that *two*, if your backbone and pelvis are built that way, like ours."

She gazed at me a minute. Then she shrugged. "Readers expect extra legs, and different-colored races, too. I mean, here we have red, and copper, and bronze, and yellow, and brown and black, and white —hm?"

I was shaking my head. "Ain't no white folks on earth, except albinos. We 'white' folks are pink, or tan, some of each or take your choice. And we spend lots of money and time trying to get darker to look more like people we've been kicking around ever since some ass ran onto Africa. Why not postulate really white people? I mean *white*."

She shrugged, jerking her head. "On a warm young planet? Nonsense. Green or blue, I think. That's about all we don't have on Earth."

"They sound either necrotic or putrid to me," I said. "Besides, they've both been used, over and over.

Carter even put giant blue men on ancient earth—identical with those Bradbury put on Mars as substitutes for ERB's unjolly green giants."

She regarded me awhile, then said, "You sure do try to make it hard for a girl to write a simple s&s story, Henry Ardor!"

"Sorry. I was just trying to get you to do something different, for a change. What about the ladies—what we talked about before. Chattel?"

She sighed. "I guess they'll have to be. I mean, having them treated the way we like to think Arthur's knights did is ridiculous. But—I won't spend much time on that, and I will show that it's perfectly normal for women to be as lusty as men, and to heck with St. Paul!"

I laughed. "Attagirl!"

"Well, it won't be all that easy for my hero, though," Evelyn said, watching her swinging foot. Any mention of sexuality always had her swinging her foot. I wondered if her toes were curling in those business-like flats she wore. "None of this dropping down, finding a beautiful doll menaced by beasties or baddies, and handily killing them with his mighty blade and increased agility—although I *am* going to have Afrodyte lighter; he needs *some* help. Anyhow, none of that coincidence stuff, and none of this princesses-running-around-getting-kidnapped-but-never-raped-and-rescued-and-rerescued, either. My hero has to *think*, and create his own darned kingdom."

I grinned. "Ah. He IS going to have a kingdom?"

"Oh yes. Eventually . . . in about the second or third book, I guess. Anyhow, it's all always just too ridiculously convenient for the lone Earthman on where-have-you, and *I'm* going to be *different*."

"Why don't you try writing one from the female

viewpoint, Ev? I mean—with a female protagonist. A heroine, rather than a hero."

"Dullsville," she answered at once, thereby giving me some psychological insight into Evelyn Shay. "Besides—what would she *do*? Run around getting raped all the time? I'm not writing THAT kind of story!"

"Someone should," I muttered, looking at the ceiling. "I bet it would sell like crazy! Joanna Carter, maybe, sort of a tomboy, and she gets raped a lot, and captured and all that, but finally finds a bunch of amazons and becomes boss—"

Again she shrugged. "See? Same old plot."

"I guess," I said, and I reached for a cigarette. "You going to make the hero think a little, huh? That'll be unique. A mystery or two?"

"Oh yes! I'm working on that part now—as soon as my hero Achilles Caxton arrives, he gets some cryptic stuff laid on him. And—"

The scene faded from my mind. On Aros, in Brynda, in Mama Selapah's, I sat up on the strawticked bed. I stared at the wall opposite.

The hero would have to think—like wondering what the hell was going on all the time, and trying to dope out things rather than plunging in. Things would be tougher for the hero—like finding a local citizen—a dying one. Like rescuing a girl—who vanished. There would be monsters, colored ones: like gray-blue, six-legged slooks and blue-gray, basketball-dunker Vardors. There would be the rape to be expected in a barbar society—but the ladies would like it. As the Jadiriyah Solah had, broadcasting her orgasmic ecstasy, as Dejah Thoris apparently would, hurt and shook because I hadn't accepted Julan. An easily-learned universal language—ridiculous, but necessary to a wandering hero, unless he picked up languages

in a few hours, like Tarzan. And a cryptic message:
such as *Hai azul thade cor zorveli nas!*

"My god! Is that it? *Am I a character in Evelyn's
novel?*"

And a few minutes later:

"My god! What if I'm not the hero? Or what if
Evelyn never finishes it—will I just—freeze?"

And a few minutes after that:

"But if I *am* the hero—is the plot all worked out?
Can I be killed? Am I a *person,* freewilled ole Hank
Ardor, or am I just a character, a chessman manipu-
lated by Evelyn Shay? And if she *does* finish it,
will I just freeze then? Or live happily ever after?
—Or dear god, will I have to spend the rest of my life
chasing around after every bad guy who kidnaps my
wife once a month and twice in leap year?"

I groaned. I snarled. I cursed. My heart speeded to
a run. I began to get wet and prickly. It all fitted too
damned well. Things weren't too easy: sure, I ran onto
a native right away, and learned the language (fairly well). But he died, and there I was. Sure, I found a
damsel in distress—but AFTER she'd been distressed
even more by both Vardors, while I lay there helplessly—the perverse slapping down of the "hero" by a female writer: Evelyn Shay. Sure, I rescued said damsel
(who, come to think, looked like the woman Evelyn
Shay thought was the best looking in the world; was
Solah Evelyn Shay herself—as she'd LIKE to be?).
But then she took off, leaving me stranded—which
was a bitchy, evelynshay thing to do: again, compli-
cating things for the hero, switching the standard plot
around.

I pushed the thoughts on:

Yeah, I'd found people, and they'd accepted me,
and I had been the hero of the attack on the caravan

—I guess. At least I'd got the insurance money as re-ward. And I'd rescued still another demoiselle—again, not a princess. None of that stuff, Evelyn had said. And instead of horrifying her, turning her off with my forwardness—I had insulted and hurt her by just the opposite! Carter called Dejah Thoris "My princess," (as well as I remember) and thus insulted her. How was he to know that meant "darling-sweetheart-mine" on Mars? He was entirely too forward; boorish. The word "boor" appeared in any such novel worth its advance.

Me? The opposite: Evelyn's perversity! SHE had written the script for this story—and I hadn't read it. As a matter of fact I had read all the wrong ones!

Etc. But there were still holes. So I was a character in a novel being written by Evelyn Shay (and if I catch up, will tomorrow be delayed or called on ac-count of rain or something?) So . . . how come poor Kro Kodres looked like someone *I*'d known; it wasn't likely that Evelyn had. And how come Dejah Thoris (unimaginative scientist-type female!) looked like Sophia Loren . . . when I *knew* the number two woman Evelyn would most rather look like was Bri-gitte Bardot? ("Those are the two, Hank," she'd said. "Sure, I know they're almost opposites in color and build. But they're both beautiful, and don't make any moralistic connections. I said LOOK LIKE them, not BE or BE LIKE them!")

And what about the latest development—her father and the invitation to dinner? Come to think, Pro Thoris looked like a man I once knew. I hadn't got to *know* him—I was messing around in a tiny motor-boat on Jennie Wiley's Lake, and all of a sudden this kingsize houseboat looked as if it were about to run us down. About the time I muttered "Stand by to re-

pel boarders" (getting scared, I admit; that thing
was BIG) a voice bellowed. Upshot was the gregar-
ious M.D. on board wanted some drinking company,
and I wound up drinking his gin 'n' tonic and sitting
at the wheel of his boat. Anyhow—Evelyn *couldn't*
have known him.

Too, there was the matter of the parrot, the jungle,
the parrot-dominated men: *that* part of my picaresque
Arone adventure was as if in a story written by a
parrot, specifically Pope Borgia Bighead. And the
disappearing-reappearing jungle—what about that?"

I'd had the thought before; maybe you have. It is
the absolute height of egoism. Suppose you are the
only person, the only creature in the world. Suppose
everything else was put here for you. There's been no
history; just books and artifacts. There's no New York
(unless you live there). Just maps and newspapers
and so on. There is *nothing*—except what's right
around you. Sure, if you decide to go to New York,
it's there. THEY put it there. (Who? I don't know.
God. The Secret Masters. The Nine.) If you could
somehow disguise your intent and spin around fast
enough—there wouldn't be anything behind you. It
would snap right into existence, of course, because
you were looking. And you'd rub your eyes and think
you were going over the edge, maybe. But you
wouldn't worry about it—*unless you suspected.*

Anyhow, that way once you emerged from a jungle
it wouldn't be there anymore, and if you looked
back over your shoulder it would be gone. That
was a hole in the Evelyn-Shay-novel theory, and there
was a hole in the hole.

True, the jungle hadn't been there when I looked
back. But the desert had. And if this were *that* sort of
thing, just me, and a lot of window dressing, then

there wouldn't have been *anything* there, would there?

"Maybe I'm dreaming," I muttered, staring at the floor of Mama Selapah's. "Maybe I'm on an LSD trip. Maybe—"

No more maybes came. I thought sure I had the answer; the character-in-a-novel theory explained many of the puzzles, the inconsistencies. But—not all of them.

I lay back, wishing the Excedrin people had got to Aros (I think I had Headache Number ΦZ, in Arone numerals). I did some more ceiling-staring.

Then I heard someone come up the steps and go down the hall, and a door closed, and I went down the hall to meet one of my fellow Guildsmen. I had a few questions. As it turned out we had two more in the room by late afternoon, all offering advice and answering questions both asked and unasked. One knew about me; he told the others; they wanted a demonstration; I jumped and hit my head on the ten-foot ceiling on the way over the bed and sprawled. Everybody laughed, then looked nervous, and I laughed, and I had three friends. They gave me more advice and answered more unasked queries.

13

The custom
that was not chivalric

Pro Thoris answered the door: "You weren't supposed to come through the shop, barbarian!" he snapped, but by then it was a joke, a pet name, and I grinned.

"How else?"

He shook his head. "America must be about the size of a sword scabbard! This building goes all the way through the block, couldn't you tell? My home faces on the other street."

"Oh," I said, feeling jubilant, and I smiled and walked off.

"Ardor—"

I went around the block and then realized I hadn't counted buildings. I was just going to knock on a strange door and ask which house was Pro Thoris' when the door to the adjacent house opened. "Over here, you stupid barbarian!"

"You certainly talk snotty to a strong young Guildsman, you old tin-tinkerer." He was that kind of man; every now and then you meet a person who is real, who exists as he is rather than within and behind a mask or three, and within a few minutes you've been old friends for twenty years.

"I would demonstrate to you my ability with a sword," he growled, "but I would be likely to forget myself and use it on your backside, which would be unseemly for both of us."

"Talk talk talk. Where is the loveliest girl in Brynda?"

"In the kitchen. You think I have servants? You think she lives a life of leisure? She keeps house, cooks, and helps in the business."

I turned around and cocked an eye at him. "And what are you going to do when I take her away from you?"

Those melted-chocolate eyes studied me for a moment. Then: "Have you considered giving up your violent life of the sword and becoming an apprentice silversmith?"

It was my turn to study his face. Perfectly open; almost an ingenuous face in the honesty and straight-forwardness of its expression. I shook my head. "I have no artist in me, Thoris, and no craftsman either. Think about it. You'd better either consider a house-keeper, a slave, or a remarriage. Say, do you know Mama Selapah?"

He didn't bother to answer, merely nodding to a short, too-low couch covered with an intricately-worked drape; it reminded me of the Islamic countries of Earth. I wondered if there was one single flaw, the deliberate mistake made because only Allah is perfect. I sat. The wine pitcher and goblets were before me. Goblets. Sunday-best! Unfinished.

"You explained?"

"What? To whom?"

"Don't play that sweet innocent game with me, prince of silversmiths! You know what, and to whom."

He smiled, we nodded at each other across the brims of our goblets, and he drank. I waited. I didn't want to interrupt between question and answer by having to make some pleasant comment about the wine.

"I explained."

I waited. Then: "You're going to make me ask. All right. I ask. And—"

He shrugged. "Women are women, and girls are girls, but their minds are unreadable as the stars," he said, which is better in Arone, since it rhymes and scans.

I was full of advice and thoughts and vinegar, and I barely contained myself until Dejah Thoris appeared to announce dinner. Yes, she still looked like Her; even better, now, with her face clean and her hair kempt and coiffed. She filled to perfection a loose gown of sky blue, girt with a white sash whose ends fell past her knees. The hem caressed her feet, which were bare.

I deposited my goblet, rose quickly, and went straight to her.

"Dejah Thoris: I apologize profusely to the comeliest girl in all Brynda for the barbaric ignorance of a stranger here, and I lay claim to Julan within the period of the nearer moon."

She stared at me. Those large, long eyes were at first wide, then slowly narrowing, as her mouth widened just as slowly into a smile.

"I didn't know you could speak so prettily," she said. "And I see that you've been about learning our customs, but it's 'within the period of the *biggest* moon.' "

Oops; I had accidentally performed a mental translation of the ritual phrase I had just learned. "Within the period of the bigger moon," I said quickly, and smiled, and her smile went wider and there was life and electricity or stars or something in her eyes; whatever it is that makes them seem to sparkle with inner lights.

She bowed her head. "I renew offer to my savior," she said, which was also ritual, and then she looked up and added, "But you haven't even seen all the girls in Brynda." Which was not ritual, but really is, in a way, on Earth as it is on Aros. It's an ancient ritual performed by a woman who's had one compliment and would like another: it's called fishin'.

"Time for that later," I said.

"Good then," Pro Thoris said just behind me. "Then let's eat, and we can take our time, and you can drink a lot, since you'll be spending the night."

Which I admit weakened my knees somewhat and played absolute hell with my appetite, even if the food was good. I admit to some (stupid) embarrassment.

Out there on the desert, immediately after I'd got her away from that Vardor, would have been one thing: spontaneous. Here it was another matter. There sat daddy, and there sat the lovely, bosomy girl with whom I was going to spend the night, and it was . . . different. The spontaneity was gone, and he'd be here, probably in the next room, and suddenly I was drinking first wine and then the after-dinner distilled wine of Azulthade—brandy, and good—and wondering if I would embarrass myself with a bad case of psychic impotence.

After one brandy in the living room Pro Thoris came suddenly to his feet. "I'll have to hurry—you should have reminded me, Dejah. It's Farsday, and I'm going to be late. Rethah will be beside herself." He left the room, returning almost at once with a lot of dark blue cloak.

"Uh—pardon me . . . but who's Rethah?"

"Father's mistress," Dejah Thoris said, as if it were a stupid question.

Pro Thoris paused at the door to glance back: "My *Farsday* mistress, girl; don't demean me before the barbarian!" And he winked and left. A moment later the door reopened and his head appeared, black and white and bald. "May Krotis smile and Thahara frown," he said, grinning, rolling his eyes from me to Dejah, and then he was gone.

This time he stayed gone, and I wondered what Rethah looked like. For that matter, I wondered what his Sajaday mistress looked like—and if he had one for every other night in the week.

It was That Time, and he who hesitates is lost, and so on, and I had received advice and coaching aplenty from my three fellow-denizens of Mama Selapah's. Not without some trepidation, I stood and crossed to her. I drew her up from her couch; she came willingly.

"You are beautiful, Thorisan Dejah."

She smiled a quiet, closed-mouth smile. It was irresistible; her lips were irresistible. I kissed her, and quickly learned not only that the custom exists on Aros, but that Dejah knew quite well how to perform it. Our hands tightened about each other gradually, mine moving, moving, stroking her through the soft, rather filmy fabric of her gown. I was very aware of a large amount of soft but shockingly firm bosom pressing into me, someplace between my chest and stomach.

After awhile her hand went back, found mine. She twined our fingers, then turned, and I allowed myself to be led into a room I had not previously entered: hers. It was soft and lovely and dim, only partially illuminated by the light filtering in from the living room. I still had her hand, and I pulled her back to me, against me. My hands moved lightly over the flare of her hips and the sudden inrushing tininess of her waist, up over the swell of her ribcage and then I was cupping, carefully and tenderly, the softness of her breasts through her gown.

The mounds within the fabric were stiff-tipped; those tips stiffened still more as I greeted them with my fingertips. Her eyes were closed, her head thrown back, and her hands, too, were moving. I am not sure how, or how long it took: not long. We undressed each other. We did it as if we had known each other for years, as if we'd been doing this for years. Then, holding her, I moved forward, and she backed the few short steps to her pastel-covered, pillow-strewn bed. The soft pillows and spread caressed us as we twined, but their caress was no softer than her hands on me. I stroked her arms, her flanks, her breasts, and over the smooth little mound of her belly. My hand slipped lower, rubbing and exploring. Her mouth drifted open, her eyes closed. Her thighs seemed to part without motion. Her hands were on me, on my shoulders, on my back, pulling, pulling as she writhed. We caressed each other's lips, moving and caressing all the while, and then our lips could no longer caress but sought to crush and bite and enter, teeth and tongues entering strongly into the action. Her legs had drifted further and further open, until I lay between them, and it was necessary to move forward only a little.

I moved forward a little, and eventually a good deal further, and I have absolutely no intention of giving you a free ride with any further talk of Dejah and me and that first time.

I spent the night, and we enjoyed each other again in the morning, and I left, without knowing whether Thoris had returned or not.

When I returned just after noon the shop was padlocked and they were gone.

14.
The woman who
used to be a witch

"Thoris and his sexy daughter? You ought to know, Guildsman! Guildchief Shayhara's personal squadders came and took them both away. Can't you see the seal on the door?"

I stared at the man, the proprietor of a curio shop across the narrow street from the Thoris shop. "Whaaat? What *for?*"

He shrugged, raising two hands, palms up. "The Guildchief doesn't confide in me, Guildsman. Doesn't he in you?"

I'm afraid I acted pretty much like a uniformed snot: I bent down and got a nice handful of his tunic and pulled him up from his tailor's squat before his shop door. His eyeballs threatened to pop forth and clutter his round little cheeks.

"No," I snarled, "he doesn't, and you'd be better advised to keep your nasty little tongue still!" Then I realized he was staring *past* me, not at me. I swung around—just in time to get a facefull of flapping green wings as my peregrinating parrot returned, backflapping to touch down on my shoulder.

"Hey, Hank!"

"Hey yourself, Bighead!"

"The bird talks—you answer—you are the foreigner Ardor?"

I turned back to face the man whose tunic I still grasped. I nodded. "I am. What about it?"

"I apologize for my tone to you, Ardor! You're the man rescued Pro's daughter from the perfidious Var-

dors. There's not a man in Brynda doesn't love both
of them, especially Dejah!" He shook his head with a
reminiscent sigh. Then his eyes widened again, probably seeing something in mine I didn't know was
there. "You must know she transacts much of his
business outside the shop—he never leaves except at
night, that great lover Pro Thoris! Think of our
pleasure in *watching* her; think of every man's regard
for you for saving her, and our envy of you, after last
night."

"What about last night?"

He smiled. "Julan!"

And without even a morning newspaper or Paul
Harvey! News is news, and it travels, no matter
what the communications situation!

I released him, apologized—admittedly brusquely
—and asked him again what he knew of the arrest of
Pro and Dejah Thoris.

He shook his head. "I don't. There are rumors.
Listen, let me call inside to my worthless daughter,
who will mind the shop—badly—while I take you to
meet Lalaikah. She knows everything."

He did, the chubby little fellow, and I followed his
rapid little footsteps down the street—exchanging
greetings constantly—and around the corner and
along another street and into a dingy old place whose
whitewash was peeling.

The room was dim, the incense strong, the candles
smoking to make the eyes water. The furniture and
once-elegant draperies and once-rich rug were old,
very old and fading. And so was the woman who sat
in the center of the carpet, tailor-fashion as my guide
had sat. I think; she was covered from just beneath
the chin in black, a tentlike dress that flowed down to
lie in ripples on the carpet about her. It left bare no
part of her save her head. The head was long of

chin, sparse of hair, gaunt and fine-etched with so many wrinkles it resembled a piece of paper wadded angrily into a ball and then straightened. And she was nearly as pale. Her eyes were keen, though, and seemingly younger than her face. Her voice was a firm, throaty alto, shockingly deep.

She was Lalaikah, formerly jadiriyah to the temple and now a has-been, forbidden to leave her street and her house after dark on pain of death from the Guild that had supplanted her.

"You bring a Guildsman here, Nammis? You are old and senile before your time!" And she stared at me with unsheathed contempt and hate.

"A man in a Guildsman's uniform, Jadiriyah," I said, quietly and with a tone of respect. "If I were differently clothed you wouldn't stare at me in hate. I am Hank Ardor, I am a foreigner, and—"

"Ah. And Nammis has brought you here to learn why the Guildchief arrested your paramour, eh? No, no—don't dare to correct *me*, Hank Ardor of Earth! I know well that you were but offered and accepted —belatedly—Julan with Thorisan Dejah. But my word is correct—for already the skeins of your life tapestry and hers are interwoven, and the knots binding them are lover's knots. And that creature on your shoulder: if you will leave him with me, I will teach him our language within a day. Don't trouble to relay my words to him; I have already spoken to him in his mind."

And Pope Borgia lifted easily into the air from my shoulder, flapped a couple of times, and soared to the black-clad and narrow shoulder of the old woman on the rug. "She's OK, Hank!"

"Nammis: return to your shop before your giddy daughter sells the place for enough dowry to tempt a man who would flee from her scrawniness," Lalaikah said. Nammis, with a little head-bob of respect, departed. I glanced about, then hunkered down, squatting to face Lalaikah so she would not have to crack her neck looking up at me. I wondered if she ever rose from this rug, from this place, the precise intersecting point of the beautiful old rug's complicated pattern.

"You called me Hank Ardor of Earth," I said.

"Of course. How silly to call yourself 'of America'! You think too small, Hank Ardor. Your world should have outgrown nationalism; this world has barely discovered it. Yes, I know of you. I knew when you came here. It is in the carpet."

I looked at the rug. She chuckled. Naturally I saw nothing to read, and certainly I'd no idea of where to find me in its many colors and vermiform pattern and tiny intersticings of varicolored skeins.

"Then you must know *where* this is, why I am constantly dizzy with the mystery and the inconsistencies of this place."

The thin, thin head nodded. "I know. But it is for you to learn. You have clues aplenty, but I will add this one: Aphrodite is goddess of love, and Eros, too, means love and thus is connected with the goddess, and Aros is simply Eros respelled, is it not? But wait: don't speak. Save it. Your feet are on the road that leads to your destiny. You came to ask of Dejah Thoris—how easily you men forget, even when you tell yourselves you are 'in love,' whatever idiocy that phrase may convey to your superstitious and romantic little mind! Listen."

I listened. I had no intention of doing anything else. This seemingly-bodiless old woman topped any mystery I had yet encountered on Aros/Eros (/Aphrodite?).

"The jadiriyah Shayharasan Solah is a bitch," she

said. "Think about it. Her father is master of Brynda, and very nearly master of Itza and Rizathade as well. That would be enough for a spoiled and willful only child, and a daughter at that—and worse, a well-favored one. Physically, I mean. Her mind is a collection of spiderwebs and cess and cicatrices festering. I know what it is to be young and lovely and desirable, and powerful, and sickeningly spoiled, Hank Ardor. I have lived there." She laughed. Her teeth were gleaming white, although a bit too much of them showed as her gums withdrew from them with her age.

"Oh yes. I am over a hundred years old. Try to see what this face was, once, and you will know I cannot be bothered to lie. Now. Her station as Shayhara's daughter, as I said, is quite enough to make a girl a predatory serpent—but Solah is also blessed with the power of the ring. She is a jadiriyah, a sorceress—on your Earth, a witch. As I was, and, though Shayhara knows it not, still am." Her jaw tightened, then: "Although the powers left me, since he confiscated my ring and set it on his daughter's hand, are childish trifles. But still"—she smiled—"they transcend any power she might have without that ring, the ring you gave her, in your idiot's ignorance. No wait: don't say it. I know, I know. You have been a man in the dark, a man blind since you arrived here, naked and baffled. Well.

"All unwittingly you insulted Her Bitchiness, the beloved term by which we call the Jadiriyah of Brynda. In the same way you insulted Thorisan Dejah, but an honest explanation sufficed to mollify both her father and herself. Not difficult, particularly in view of the fact that you wear the face of her dreams and she was all wet and trembly the moment she saw you."

"I wear—"

She smiled again. "Yes. Isn't that interesting—and she has the face of *your* dreams. Well, such things happen, upon occasion. But I assure you of this: Solah will listen to no explanations. Nor will her father, who is completely dominated by her. Yes. The master of Brynda, the chief of all warriors—clay in the clutching hands of his daughter. Is there aught so unusual in that—certainly it is not uncommon where you come from, and most particularly in your own little section of that place, America. Of *course* she was torn and sore when you found her, and bleeding too. Of *course* she desired no further tumbles. But she offered, ritually. And though you were nice enough about it, you refused—and *you did not refuse ritually*. Had you done so you would be favored of Shayhara, and probably wear Commander's stripes or more. As it is, Shayhara learned only this morning that you were in the Guild. A problem, but it stands you well: you'd have been killed as Hank Ardor. As Guildsman First Hank Ardoris you have certain rights."

"I want to know what they are, Jadiriyah," I told her. "But—what of Dejah and her father?"

One bony shoulder rose in a shrug; the parrot teetered and made a nasty noise. Her head swiveled slowly and their eyes met and he looked away. More sorcery: a parrot is as hard to stare down as a cat. Certainly I've never succeeded.

She looked back at me. "The incense bothers you? The smoke?"

I shook my head.

"Incredible. You tell the truth when it might hurt you and you lie to avoid hurting someone else! I would like to go and live among your people, just to see and listen to them. How strange they all must be! But your question: Solah has whispered sweet evils in her father's ear. His agents searched for you. Learned that you had been accepted into the Guild, that you lodge at Selapah's. But you were not there, and they learned where you were last night. They reported to the Guildmaster as soon as he arose this morning. Perhaps his daughter was present, perhaps not, perhaps she had agents there. She has her own agents, you see, even among her father's agents and personal squad. But immediately the squadders were sent to arrest Thoris and daughter."

"Because of me."

"This smoke and stinkstuff is getting me dizzy, Hank," the parrot complained. I relayed his words to Lalaikah, and there was silence, as he looked sharply at her and seemed to be listening. Then he flew over and clutched a damper in his claws and in five tries put out all three candles. Next he closed the trapdoor lid on the censer. And he flew back to her shoulder.

"He hears me in his mind, and he obeys nicely," Lalaikah said. "He is a very intelligent bird." She was silent a moment, and he snapped his head to stare at her, then preened.

"Yes, Hank Ardor, because of you. You wronged Solah, which is worse than spitting on the Queen of Inglund." She frowned. "*England*," she corrected meticulously.

"You know my thoughts!"

A shrug: "Of course. Solah learned you were in Brynda, that you were friend of Thoris and spent the night with his daughter. So she has had them arrested. You will have several choices, now." She hesitated; I waited; she smiled. "A good trait, though dangerous with a woman: we like our little moments of drama, and want you to ask 'Ah? What are they?' and the like. But here are your choices:

"You can flee Brynda."

"I will not."

"Of course not. That would be the sensible action, and you are a man, and an unduly romantic one. You've read far too many books, Hank Ardor. Life might well be simpler for you had both you and Evelyn Shay read less. Well, then, here's another choice: you could try to free Thoris and Thorisan Dejah by force. Ah, I see that appeals to you, you poor ass of a man!"

"Jadiriyah: it is cowardly of one who is gifted with both powers and the wisdom of ages to play name-calling with a young man with a normal brain and a little muscle."

She gazed at me, then laughed. "Which is why Pro Thoris thinks so highly of you—you rapped him, I wager, just as firmly. You are right, and I have no need to aggrandize myself by smiting you with words. Nor does it become me. No one should call one names but oneself, eh?"

I was silent. She was silent; finally I decided to shelve that exchange by returning to business: "Is it possible?"

She shook her head. "Of course not. If you commanded a thousand Guildsmen, protectors all, you could not free them by force."

"In that case I hope there are more choices."

"There are. Now listen. I am going to speak in your mind, and your friend here will hear also. I will call him Pope Borgia, not Bighead. I've no proof he deserves such a title. It means someone very brainy here, you know. We might call Sorah 'Bighead.'"

There was not a movement in that incense-creeping room, and not a sound. But we listened.

Oh. She looked like my grandmother, by the way.

15

The woman who
still was a witch

How, I thought, tramping down that long purple carpet, *am I to do it? Oh, the old girl told me what I must do—but not how. Now how the holy hell does a man—a man, and nothing more, even if I have always thought it was quite a bit—match wits and powers with a bonafide certified witch?*

And I hadn't even a dog, a scarecrow, a lion, and a woodman, tin or otherwise.

But I walked that long carpet two days after my conversation—onesided conversation! with the ex-Jadiriyah of Brynda, and at the narrow purple strip's other end was a dais, and on the dais sat, as if enthroned custodians of empire, the Guildmaster of Brynda and his witch-daughter.

I had made my appeal; it had been granted because there was no other course to Shayhara, and now here I was for my audience/trial. Present were representatives of the Crown and the Merchants' Guild and the Artisans' and four scribes. One would record all Shayhara's words; another mine, another Solah's. The fourth would scratch down anything said by anyone else.

(The Crown: a figurehead, of course, living a sterile life in his magnificent palace, surrounded by Guildsmen for protection and as spies, allowed to poke out his face now and again to crown his son as heir, or dedicate this or that, or proclaim this or that, or say something sweet and innocuous. Yet he was revered, that powerless man, him and his family, for he and his house were a lasting symbol, a slender thread of gold connecting past and future and present. And when Nero sent his commands to the Senate there was still the pretense that they were the power in Rome, in a precisely opposite situation. Here people called themselves a kingdom while being ruled by several guilds—which were in turn dominated by one guild, it dominated by one man, and him by one lovely girl with the face of an American actress.)

"Hank Ardor of America, Guildsman First." The words came from the Stentor to my left as I arrived at the stripe across the purple carpet beyond which I could not step. I halted and bowed my head, briefly, before looking up at the Guildmaster and his daughter—the Guildmistress!

He stared back. Perhaps he was fifty, perhaps forty; I have commented that people tend to age faster here. He was entirely bald, I was told, and the Guild scalplock was secured to his head each morning by his very personal—and very mute—valet. He was obviously a physically powerful man, his chest and arms full of muscle and his naked calves knotted with it, like a ballet dancer or a circus aerialist. He wore standard garb: one-sleeved red tunic over red trunks, short boots, bracers on his wrists. There was nothing to distinguish him as Master of the Warriors' Guild, nothing to distinguish him from a recruit such as I was. No mark, no stripes or stars or eagles or even a sash or a pen or a medallion.

But he would be recognized by every man, woman, and child in Brynda and the outlying farmlands.

"You asked for Peoples' Hearing, Hank Ardoris. Speak." His voice was a perfectly normal voice, very clear, slightly, twangily nasal, but it was a voice that carried well.

"Guildmaster, Peoples' Representatives. I am a total stranger to Brynda and the ways of Brynda. On the desert I met one Kro Kodres, a Guildsman of Brynda. He was dying, and my efforts at saving his life were to no end, although I spared him some pain. He advised me of the whereabouts of a girl, and at the time I thought 'Jadiriyah' was a name. He specified that I was to convey to her a ring. It appeared valuable, and I owed Kro Kodres nothing, but I went to seek her: on foot, on the Yellow Desert. I found her in the hands of two Vardors who would certainly have returned her as slave to their women and lustful men. I slew them both. I returned her ring to her."

"Stop." The voice came from my right; the Artisans' box. "Jadiriyah of Brynda: does this man speak true?"

"To my knowledge," she said in a voice sheathed in steel and wrapped in ice. "He has neglected only to say that I *asked* him of the ring before he returned it to me."

I waited. Shayhara nodded. "She made a statement to me that I was unfamiliar with, other than literally: 'I offer you recompense.' I thanked her. I must point out that Julan, as it exists in Brynda and this part of the world, does not exist in America. Thus I had no idea what she was offering, nor that it was ritual and that some ritual response was expected of me."

"Stop." From the Artisans again: "Pro Thoris and his daughter have both verified this. That is to say, this man had to have our custom explained to him by the silversmith of Artisan Street."

The Jadiriyah lifted one lovely shoulder in a shrug, and another inch of pale breast rippled in the deep V of her gown. "Inadmissible; the silversmith and his daughter are his friends."

It went on. I gave them the rest of my story, in little detail. There were a few interruptions that clearly indicated the Artisans were my friends, the Warriors my enemies. Sometime during that trial it occurred to me that my friend Stro Fentris was without doubt in trouble and might as well forget having his wife sew that white stripe on his tunic—or have her re-move it, more likely.

By the time it was over—with me standing there all the while, the outcome was obvious.

Look, it's true the merchants and the artisans have a great deal more in common than either of them has with the warriors. But—the artisans are more de-pendent upon the merchants than vice versa, and the merchants depend upon the Warriors Guild. If Shay-hara were to call a strike or closeout against them—they would be stolen blind and slide steadily into ruin as what caravans were sent out never returned. Even-tually none would be sent at all. Obviously the merchants and the artisans could vote down the warriors—and then Shayhara would override them in Executive Decision.

Thus I would be convicted anyhow. But—that way the merchants would be in trouble, and so naturally I knew the vote would be Merchants/Warriors against Artisans: conviction two to one of the monstrous crime of willfully insulting the Jadiriyah. Shayhara could make some sympathetic noises, but after all his hands were tied . . . (they always were, unless a vote displeased him, in which case he either vetoed or Took Sanctions or called for a new trial).

I had known all this before I requested what Bryn-da calls a Public Trial. I was here for the drama, not justice. And the time came:

"All evidence has been heard. Guildsman First Hank Ardoris, do you stand ready to hear verdict and sentence?"

I looked straight back into Shayhara's steady dark eyes, and I said "No." And there was an instant turmoil of voices and rustling of clothes as men gasped and exclaimed and moved to mutter. Solah looked shocked; her father raised his eyebrows; I smiled at Solah. Her eyes narrowed. Oh, the cruel petulance in that lovely little mouth!

"You said no?" The Guildmaster leaned forward. "I assume you will tell us why."

"I do not admit to your authority," I told him, with adrenalin going through me sufficient to power an Olympic team to victory.

He sat back. Just as he started to speak his daughter did: "WHY?"

More turmoil; heads swung and again everyone exclaimed and muttered as through one high-set and glassless window flew the green streak that was Pope Borgia. He swooped over the seated merchants, causing a few heads to jerk ludicrously down, and he came straight in and executed a marvelous landing on my right shoulder. He stared at the enthroned Guildmaster and daughter.

"Because he can't be tried by a silly stacked little court like this!" Pope Borgia screeched, in his newly —and miraculously, as far as I was concerned—acquired Arone. "He isn't just a man you can run through this comical mill ruled by one man who is ruled by one woman! Hank Ardor is a jadiriy!"

When the noise died down: "This . . . talking bird says that you are a . . . a sorcer*er*," Shayhara said, carefully, obviously never before having spoken the word without a female ending.

I nodded. "My messenger between this world and the world of shadow-power speaks true," I said.

And there was another several minutes of hullabaloo, finally stemmed by the Stentor's voice and by the Guildmaster's rising.

"There are no male sorcerers."

I shrugged. "In America there are no female sorcerers."

"Simple enough," Solah said coldly. "Let him prove his claim."

"Can Shayharan Solah converse with birds? Send them from her and call them to her? Certainly, she can appear and disappear, moving from one place to another without being seen, but can she leap twenty feet?" *Leap tall buildings with a single bound?* I thought.

"My powers are not challenged."

"Are mine?"

"Of course. You stand here a convicted criminal—"

"Ah!" I smiled. "I hope scribes are scribing. That is the first admission of what we all know: that the verdict was reached before the accused came here! I remind Shayharan Solah that I do NOT stand here a convicted criminal. I am simply an accused man who denies the power of this court to try him."

"Simple enough," came a voice from the warriors' section. "Let him challenge the Jadiriyah."

Silence, then the Guildmaster asked, "Do you challenge?"

"No, Guildmaster. I have no desire to play games with your daughter. Why should I challenge her to a contest?"

Under no circumstances, the old woman Lalaikah had said, and repeated it, *under NO circumstances are you to challenge her. It must be she who challenges you, Hank Ardor.*

Of course Solah was equally adamant, but I knew what I was about and remained cool, while she grew angrier and angrier. Consider her background and her circumstances, and you understand readily that she lost her temper and shot to her feet and shot out a lovely arm to point at me, shouting, "I challenge this man! There shall be a contest of our powers, and woe be to him if he fails to match or best!"

I bowed my head. Knees shaky, armpits trickling chill wetness down my sides, I nodded. "I cannot refuse to accept such a sweetly-put proposition from such a charming lady."

There was laughter, and someone from the Artisans' section pointed out that I was here precisely because I had found myself able to resist a previous proposition from this same lovely lady, and there was more laughter.

"To begin with," she snapped, her eyes bright and vicious, "join me!"

She grasped her ringed hand in her other, as she had done that night on the desert, and she closed her eyes. And vanished. She called out from the Warriors' section, ten feet from me—fifteen or so feet from the throne. "JOIN me, O sorcerer!"

I looked at her smiling face and the smiling faces around her, and I nodded. Carefully I stripped off my jingling medallion: a slender leather strand threaded through the ring on Dr. Blakey's chiming watch. Then, while they muttered, off came my tunic, with the parrot standing at my feet, a beady-eyed sentinel over the discarded gear.

"I call all to note that Solah"—using her name unadorned, a worse slap than my previous refusal to call her Jadiriyah—"used her ring, closed her eyes, and invisibly transported herself. I shall join her without ring or my amulets, with my eyes open and my hands open and bare, and you will see me."

I pointed dramatically to her. I knew no one could resist: they all looked at her, and I jumped. Which brought me quite a lot of loud comment: I made it without difficulty, but cut it a little close so that I jostled her as I landed. She reeled back; I shot out a hand to grip her arm—without it she'd have bounced her shapely bottom off the marble floor. As soon as she had regained her balance she slapped my hand away.

"I join you, lovely lady."

She stared at me, obviously shaken; had I jumped or hadn't I? She wasn't sure—but even so, who could have jumped so far? Not she, certainly! And not—from a flatfooted start, at least—the finest athlete in the citystate.

But she was a woman, and she had to come back with something, so she challenged me to do it naked, and that embarrassed me a little, but I came out of the red trunks and submitted to a quick examination to insure I wore no charms—or anything else.

"Bighead! Beware my landing!" I shouted, and there were grins and chuckles, and eyes wavered between the parrot I was looking at and the girl several feet from me. Because, of course, my new name for Pope Borgia was the same as their gentler nickname for their Ring wearer. And so while no one stared directly at me, and while she glared around with blazing eyes, I really tried and soared over and past Pope Borgia. Several Artisans yowled and got the hell out of the way as I came down among them. A new record; I'd tried hard to throw myself forward rather than up, and so, like a line drive between pitcher and second, I went flying across the room to the tune of about twenty-five feet. I landed just in front of the Artisans' Guild Jurors.

"Nice to be among friends," I muttered, grinning,

and then I turned from them; at least two had heard, and they quickly passed the word among their ranks. I ambled back to my clothes, ignoring the stares and exclamations. I donned the tunic. Then I walked over to retrieve my trunks. Without looking at the Jadiriyah—whom my peripheral vision told me had blown her cool and was staring at me like a bug-eyed child at the circus (ouch; nasty choice of analogy)—I picked up my trunks. As calmly as possible, I donned them.

It is not an action conducive to calmness or to aplomb, struggling into one's underwear before an audience staring at absolutely no one else.

Then I milked it a little; I told Pope Borgia—in English—to bring me my medallion, which he did, and I walked back to stage center and bowed to the Guildmaster—at whose side, in a fingersnap, stood his daughter.

"Is it permissible that I now ask my challenger to perform her feat naked?" I asked.

There was a deadly silence. Looking apoplectic, Solah sat. Her father stared at me, looking as if he wished he were in Wappinger Falls. At last, quietly, painfully, he said, "It is."

"Father!"

"I decline," I said. "I have already seen the lady naked." And I bowed.

Which got me more laughter and dirty looks; I was grandstanding, of course, and enjoying myself immensely. She had broken or overlooked the Law, and I had gone along with it and bested her, and now I had done it again, with words.

Someone finally remembered to mention the Law, but not until she had extended a finger and said, "Enough of these . . . calisthenics! I defy you to—"

"Stop!" Which was a nice rule they had; at any

time during the proceedings anyone could bark
"Stop!" and the speaker, no matter who, shut up or a
mistrial was called. Looking surprised and if possible
even angrier, Solah shut up. She and her father
glared to my left. The voice had come from the
Artisans.

"We act like the barbarians the Jadiriyah has accused this man of being," the aged voice said. "Will
no one so say, not even the Master of the Guild of
Warriors of Brynda? Then I do: the Jadiriyah has
challenged. The choice of tests is up to Hank Ardor."

True, and no one could disagree, and they all looked
at me in silence, waiting for me to state my terms.
And I stood there fingering my medallion, and then
I had it.

"First, our trial will take place in the Market
Square," I said, "where there are no walls and no
question of chicanery." *And a lot bigger audience*,
I thought. "At the fifth hour of morning. I will perform a few feats, simple in America, and I will not
ask the Jadiriyah," and here I bowed as respectfully
as I spoke; I'd been a skunk long enough, "to best
any of them, but only to duplicate, precisely, each."

The Guildmaster nodded. "Do you agree?" he asked
his daughter.

Naturally she had no choice. Naturally she agreed.
I was released into the custody of Stro Fentris—
who was not, indeed, wearing the white stripe on his
tunic hem.

16.
A ball-point
and a chiming watch

It was a *lovely* day in Brynda on Aros. Pale little clouds nudged each other like pressed marshmallows in that weirdly-lighted sky. All about the Market Square and in the windows of every surrounding building people nudged each other for viewing room.

I had asked that Pro Thoris and Dejah be released: denied. I had asked to visit them: denied. I had also decided on a dramatic entry, and waited until the Jadiriyah appeared, amid great oohing and aahing, in the circle of onlookers. She was on the platform once used for hawking wares—people, mostly—in the city's younger days and preserved because Arones preserve things just as Americans do. She wore bra and trunks of brilliant green, a long band of yellow cloth falling from the hip band of the trunks to the ground between her feet. A piece of matching yellow was caught in the right side of her bra and went up over her left shoulder, to flutter behind her past the extraordinarily well-filled seat of her trunks. And of course she wore her ring, with her mass of black hair drawn back and bound with several slender fillets of gold.

She looked around. "Well? Where is the so-called sorcerer of America? Must we all wait in the sun for his appearance?" And thus she won the first point, and the first laughs.

Standing beside me, Stro Fentris' son raised an arm, and Pope Borgia saw it and swooped down from his perch atop a tall building. He landed beside the girl, amid a lot of crowd noises, strutted about, then sprang again into the air.

"I shall fetch my master," he squawked, and persuading the swell-headed little monster to say that had been the hardest part of the plan—so far. Naturally all eyes followed his brilliant green flight as he flew away, screeching "Master, Master, the girl you rescued from Vardor slavery waits!"

His flight, as planned, was away from me. Stro and his son and a couple of others and I, all hooded as were many of the crowd against the sun, had got ourselves into the center of the press, about ten feet from the platform. It was a tight-pressed crowd. But inasmuch as all of us wore vast amounts of padding to make us a little group of overfed watchers, there was plenty of room. The padding piled up at my feet; I doffed my cloak and squatted and jumped, before the crowd could start filling up the space.

It was a near thing. I came within an ace of missing the platform. But since the Jadiriyah, like everyone else, was watching the aerial antics of the supposedly-searching parrot, I recovered without much notice being taken—and incidentally made her jump a foot and squeal to boot. Neither was missed by the crowd.

I bowed to her. She lifted her chin and gave me a go-to-hell look, and then damned if we didn't have to stand there in the sun while a Stentor read every word of yesterday's proceedings. Listening, realizing the whole business had not been at all tampered with, I began to forget the sun. It was mighty favorable to my cause, letting everyone hear all that, and letting it build me up while weighing heavier and heavier on Solah's handsome shoulders.

Then it began.

"I call to note that my bird and I converse, and assume that that is a feat the Jadiriyah cannot hope to match—therefore I will not allow it to be considered," I said, grandstanding again. "And I believe both of us are weary of movement games, which the Jadiriyah has rightly termed 'calisthenics.' Nor will I ask her to attack and slay three Vardors, as I did in defending the caravan a few days ago—or to attack and slay two, as when I rescued the naked Jadiriyah from the two whose captive she was on the desert —that night I graciously returned to her her ring of power."

She gritted her teeth.

"Those are warriors' feats, and bouncing about from this location to that, whether it's from here to the Guild Headquarters or to Itza, are merely sorcerer's—I mean sorceresses, we are led by men where I came from—tricks of—calisthenics. So." I turned a little, gazing about at those many, many faces, and at the many, many faceless sun-cowls. I wore a little less than she: white trunks (in which I hoped to have a fly made; god, what a barbarous oversight!) and soft low boots and my "medallion."

"I also have no wish to tax either the Jadiriyah or the great but hot people of Brynda," I said, smiling, which won me a few smiles and a chuckle or two and a little more sympathetic audience. "Thus this will be a short test of our skills. I admit in advance that the Jadiriyah undoubtedly possesses *skills* I do not, just as I have some little powers she might find . . . difficult." With a smile at her. But there was a little noise, a murmur, and it was time for business.

"I CALL FOR MY WAND OF POWER!" I shouted, and then bellowed out "MISSISSIPPI, KENTUCKY, LOS ANGELES, CINECITTA, AND RUMPELSTILSKIN!"

And down came Pope Borgia with my pen—or rather, Dr. Blakey's pen, that lovely golden smear-proof ball-point he had sent here ahead of me—not knowing the sorcerous use to be made of it.

I was the challenged, and seemed to be in charge, so I called a fellow up out of our audience to examine the slender pen. His neighbors had to thrust him forward, of course, but he examined the "golden wand" with care and handed it back with a shrug. I asked for a public noticeboard, which is a strip of carefully prepared white hide stretched taut on a wooden frame. It is used, obviously, for the purpose of hanging up notices to the public. Good tidings and bad, proclamations, promotions, news from Itza, the like.

While everyone wondered what I was about I screwed out the pen's point—it is easy to do with one hand, and I thank the Cross people for that! Had it been one of those click-top pens my man from the audience certainly would have discovered that fact —and the point. The small bit of wax I'd put on the joint last night prevented his turning it by accident. It came off very easily, as I took the pen from him.

I stepped up to the "easel" and, with a flourish and a little muttering, printed a message: "On this day the Jadiriyah of Brynda was defeated by Hank Ardor, Sorcerer of America, as befits the relation of a man and a maid."

I stepped back, had the Stentor read it aloud (a lot of those people were too far back to read—and many of them couldn't read anyhow). There were some hoots and snorts, and some laughter and some head-wagging: some male Yeahhhs! at the sentiment of my brief message. I popped the pen into Pope Borgia's beak. He took off to flap his circuitous course to a gentleman from the Street of Artisans who waited several blocks away.

I bowed to the audience and to my opponent. Then I turned and reversed the noticeboard. I gestured, bowed again, and stepped back.

Thank god! I had not been *sure* she couldn't write with her finger or something. But the look on her face told me I had triumphed.

She tried: "This is a test of *sorcery?*"

I shrugged. "Produce your wand," I said, "and write. Or any other instrument—although not, of course, a quill and ink!" And I grinned, and got a few more laughs.

She looked fulminous—and regal; she had some control, after all. "The power," she said in a loud voice, "lay in the instrument, not in the wielder! I admit I cannot duplicate this so-called feat without having in my hand the same instrument."

"No fair," someone called, and someone else shouted "he wins, he wins!" and still another very male voice bellowed "Can she write at all?" and even her partisans couldn't help laughing.

I turned about, frowning. "The power is NOT in the instrument," I told them and her, "as we shall see. Perhaps I have won this test, and perhaps I have not. But I shall deny my beautiful opponent no opportunity to prove . . . ah, female superiority."

I shouted for Pope Borgia. He returned—oh, his flapping back and forth was a great addition to the circus, let me tell you. Anyhow back he came with the pen, only slightly altered: its cartridge was removed, its barrel stuffed with clay with a drop of silver on top, so that it would appear to be solid. A hell of a way to treat a superb writing instrument, but—rectifiable, I hoped, and certainly necessary. I handed

it to the gentleman from the audience. He examined it
with care and pronounced it to be the same, and un-
changed. Yes, the wax was back around the seam. I
handed it to the Jadiriyah.

She turned it over and over, eyeing it, and at last
grasped her ring and did some closed-eyed muttering.
Then she stepped bravely up to the blank easel and,
after several seconds of valiant endeavoring, left it as
blank as before, save for a few scratches. Ah, the
noise from our onlookers was *lovely!* Beethoven or
Rosza never sounded more beautiful to my ears.

Her fear was something she could not mask, or perhaps she forgot; it was there in her eyes and at the
white edges of her mouth. She examined the pen,
discovered the waxed seam with a sudden smile of
triumph, and had it open in a trice. She held the two
pieces high: "It's HOLLOW! Trickery!"

"Jadiriyah—PLEASE—be careful! It is for my
hand only, and—"

But about that time she interrupted with a loud
squeak, dropping both parts of the pen. As I'd feared,
the spot of silver was still warm. Not hot, but it had
startled her.

Enough; she tried it again and failed and hung her
head.

The second test: simple. My carefully-wound
pocket watch—though reversed—told me we had
consumed fifty-one minutes in test and proceedings
reading. I asked the location of the nearest sundial
and was told that there was one on the other side
of the Square—as I had learned last night. I looked at
my opponent.

"Can you control time, Jadiriyah? Think well before you answer."

She stared at me. Then she took the bull by the
horns: "Of course not!"

"Can you foretell its passage—to the instant?"

She hoisted her chin. She knew damned well no one could do that, and I knew that not even Lalaikah could or ever had. There were water clocks and hourglasses everywhere, and quite a few sundials, but no one operated on any sort of strict time schedule. "And come back for dinner!" Pro Thoris had said —without specifying a time. The dinner hour was the dinner hour; if anyone tried specifying an invitation ("Dinner will be at half after the seventeenth hour," or the like) others would have thought him unsane. Certainly, time was noted, and recorded, and historians would write that at the fifth hour (counting from sunrise) on the three hundred eighty-sixth day of the City did the Jadiriyah of Brynda meet in contest Sorcerous with the foreigner named Ardor.

It occurred to me that day that water clocks, hourglasses, *and* sundials could be made into alarm clocks, although it's trickier with sundials. Anyhow, there are now alarm clocks all over Brynda, and elsewhere, too; we did a pretty good business in them before others started making them, elsewhere. My first little factory made me wealthy.

But that's ahead of the story, and Solah and I stood on the platform that day years ago, and I promised her and the assembled crowd that I would call the precise moment of the hour's end. Further, I would be advised of it by my amulet, which I held aloft. I let her examine it (carefully; if she'd dropped it I'd have been chin-deep in hot soup). She tapped the crystal and looked at me with fear and respect, and I smiled.

"Call it off, Jadiriyah of Brynda," I urged in a low, low voice. "Drop charges. Release Pro and Dejah Thoris. You needn't even concede. Just get out of it. You've already lost more respect than most people can build in ten years, and you're about to lose it all. You'll still be Jadiriyah, of course, but—we're about to prove my superiority."

She stared at me. Her fist closed over the watch. Suddenly fearful, I stepped back and extended my hand so that all could see. She had to place it in my palm then, and though I grasped it with both hands, it apparently did not occur to her that dropping it would break it. There was no such precision machinery on Aros, of course.

"You are so sure—"

"I am," I muttered. "At precisely the moment the hour ends I will call it—can *you?* Or if we then wait for another hour to pass—will you be able to call its end?"

She looked me up and down. "Will you apologize for your behavior to me on the desert?"

"I have. Privately and publicly."

"Why did you refuse?"

"You know very damned well, Solah." There was a lot of muttering by now; we two stood in stage center with our heads close. What, the throng of course wondered, was up?

"I knew both Vardors had ravished you; I *felt* it, through your thoughts. I was too far away to get there in time to stop them; I would have if I could. And if that had happened and you had offered— even though I know nothing of the custom, I'd have been all over you. You know very well you're one of the best-looking women in the world. First, then, I declined from pure consideration for you. Had I known the ritual words, I'd have added them. And secondly—well, your experience was in my mind so that I *felt* it, including your peaks, and I assume you know how men are. I climaxed too."

"I see." She looked me up and down. "You are not ugly, you are a strong and a mighty warrior, and I think you are truthful—honorable. And—you do have the power. Or perhaps it's the bird, but no matter—the bird obeys you." She raised her eyes to my eyes, and I received a shock that transcended all the others I'd had since falling into Dr. Blakey's blasted machine.

"Julansee," she said. "But—permanently."

I let that one filter in slowly, and finally, stupidly, unsure, asked her: "Are you talking about marriage?"

The eyes flashed: "Of course! I'll be no man's mistress!"

I stood there, full of little needles and suddenly sweating again and aware that I would make some very interesting EKG peaks—if there were such an animal as an electrocardiogram anywhere within a few million million miles of Aros.

It's power, I thought. *She's boss-lady in Brynda. You have some power, and you represent a challenge to her—a long-term one. She wants an alliance. You ain't ugly, but even if you were a hideous, five-foot leper, she's willing to make the supreme sacrifice in order to ally the powers—and gain all of it. And when she knows about the pen and the watch and the parrot and whatever else, as she eventually would, then what?*

The parrot, I thought, held the answer. Pope Borgia. What happened to the husband Cesare and the Borgia Pope allied Lucrezia with in marriage, when he wasn't useful anymore, when a new alliance was more profitable? Cesare knocked him off. Maybe Lucrezia cried and maybe she didn't. But she married the next man they told her to. In this case it's worse, even more dangerous, because in this case this lovely doll herself controls the Borgia power—and once she knows and has yours, you are nothing, Hank Ardor. Nothing, except a corpse shortly mourned and soon forgot.

Behind us, the natives were getting mighty restless. "Can we discuss it later?" I asked, and I saw the look in her eyes, and knew I might as well have said "No." More honorable for me, and just as much an affront to Solah Borgia. I watched the well-separated and over-developed halves of her chest expand as she drew in a great angry breath. I glanced at the watch. *Tough, Solah baby. It's time. We can't even parley.*

It had been only eight-point-something minutes, but to the audience that was a long time. The only thing that would have kept us from being plastered with tomatoes, had they had any, was her status among them. Slipping . . . slipping . . .

I looked at her. "IS IT TIME, SOLAH? IS THE HOUR AT AN END?"

There was panic in her eyes. "Ye—no . . . "

"ARE YOU SURE?"

Panic, mounting; fear, overwhelming anger, becoming paramount, her nostrils flaring, her lips pale, her face paling, pupils dilating, a little tic in her left jaw—oh lord, she was beautiful, absolutely beautiful! Why is a woman so beautiful to us when she is scared half to death, or in pain or panic—are we so barbaric?

"I DON'T KNOW HE HAS ME GOT TO WIN CAN'T LET HIM—" It was her mind, not her throat, that hurled out those "words." The broadcast power is seldom used here. She had done so deliberately, on the desert, hoping to call in help. Now—stress. She forgot, and she broadcast. Many others heard her and knew what I knew: she was in a panic. And—

She vanished. Although I couldn't see it beyond the

great throng, I pointed in the direction of the sundial. And—their murmur rose to a cry as they all saw her. She materialized at the sundial just as they turned.

She looked up with those wide panicky eyes and saw: nothing but other eyes, staring at her, seeing her fear, her absolute terror of losing, of being thrust down and back. It was a frozen moment. She, the child caught with its hand in the cookies. The crowd, the shocked, the surprised, the slowly angering mother. For they realized what she was doing, what I'd shown them, what she'd been forced to do by being incompetent to compete. While all eyes were on the platform she meant to check the sundial and appear again almost before she was missed. Now, caught, she neither moved nor vanished. She just stared, as if hypnotized with fear. A frozen moment—but not in time. I glanced at the watch and I raised both arms high and bellowed with all the strength in my lungs and larynx:

"NOW! LISTEN! I ANNOUNCE THE TIME TO YOU WITH SHADOWORLD CHIMES! IT . . . IS . . . THE . . . FIFTH HOUR!"

And as they all stared at me in breathless silence, the amulet on my chest chimed the hour.

In the instant before pandemonium someone yelled, from the sundial: "It is TRUE! The hour BEGINS!"

The girl in the green bra and trunks vanished from the sundial. She did not reappear on the platform, or anywhere else she could be seen; she sent herself to her room in the palace, I suppose. Leaving behind her the screaming thought-concept:

HATE

And I stood there trembling, sweat streaming, staring out at all those faces until I saw a blue hood thrown back and a man raised his hand and shouted:

"Hail the Sorcerer of Brynda!"

It was my caravan friend, Thro Alnaris. His raised hand signaled his success: Dejah and Pro were out of the dungeons. Which, as we later learned, was precisely where her serene witchship had gone, stopping off at her room only long enough to collect a dagger.

17

The answer that was true— but STILL didn't satisfy

She was the Jadiriyah. She had been the Jadiriyah since she was a child. She was undefeated and unde-featable, willful and arrogant. And defeated, but un-able to accept defeat.

It began within minutes. As soon as she found the dungeons minus the two on whom she'd have let off the steam of her spite.

The sky went black. I don't think she controlled the heavens; I think it was illusion. Thunder rolled and crashed and lightning leaped and speared. The wind grew and grew and grew and eventually there was darkness, the darkness of night amid a howling, angry wind that sent dust and litter scurrying about from street to street and signs swinging and clattering. It pulled and pushed and toppled people, until they cleared the streets and battened down to shudder and roll their eyes.

We sat in Lalaikah's dark, worn-carpeted room: Dejah and Pro Thoris, and Proby and Thro and I —and the parrot, complaining, and the woman who had been a witch. She sat with her eyes closed. She'd sworn that she alone was saving the entire city from the destruction willed by Solah's rage.

Pro Thoris nudged me. "I'd think the Jadiriy of Brynda would stop all this," he muttered.

"Shut up," I said. Quietly.

"No way to talk to your father-in-law," he grumbled.

"Hush," Dejah said. "You aren't that yet, and he could change his mind!"

I squeezed her to let her know there wasn't a chance.

Outside, the wind did its absolute damndest to huff and puff and blow the city down. And then the pounding wasn't that of the loose shutter next door. It was at Lalaikah's door.

Proby and I flanked the door with drawn swords; Thro opened it. We stared at the two cloak-swathed men who were blown stumbling in, and we did not sheath our bare bodkins. They helped Thro close and bar the door.

They were Stro Fentris and the Guildmaster of Brynda.

He and I regarded each other for perhaps a minute; a very long one.

Then he swept back his cloak, to show me his sword.

"Take it," he said.

I sheathed mine without replying, and gazed at that big muscular man in silence. He looked whipped; hangdoggy.

"The girl," he said. "She's on a rampage. It's happened before, but never like this. Now the city knows what it's been like for me. The girl." He regarded the rug, then looked at me again.

"Her mother died hating me, and Solah has always hated me. But—she has the power, the jadiriyah power. I haven't been master of Brynda, or even the Guild. She has." He nodded at the door. "The street's full of serpents, now. It's . . . unbelievable. You can't make a child into a woman when you can't discipline her. When she knows she has all the power, she doesn't have to grow up. You can't teach a child control when there's no way you can discipline her, when she . . . when she can turn you about and march you into a wall, or vanish and appear behind you and slap you in the back and be gone before you turn. When she can . . . when she would make her father crow, or fall and be unable to get up."

He swung away, his face writhing in anguish. The warrior's cloak swished and flapped, low on his big calves. We said nothing, and after awhile he turned.

"They tried to slay my daughter in her spelling chamber, but she escaped. The mindtravel, of course. She's barred from our home. And I too. Stro Fentris saved me from being torn apart. I'm deposed. All . . . because of her . . . and because of my black, stinking weakness!"

Can you feel sorry for the man who's had all the power to be had over a city, more than one city?

Yes, of course, when you realize he's a man who wants to be a man but isn't; who's been pretending, all these years; who's been a self-hating puppet dangling on his daughter's—his *daughter's!*—strings.

"What will she do?" I asked.

"Kill you all! Smash this house into the bowels of the world, crush your bodies into jelly, tear the fat bosom off that horrid bitch, hang this crawling creature from the palace battlements! Strangle you with your own useless organ, Ardor!"

Solah's face was a twisted, vicious mask, her hands up and clawed even as she appeared. She still wore the green bra and trunks, and over it all a varicolored cloak that swept the floor. Her eyes seemed to burn into me, to pierce like the gale outside. Slowly she turned her ring hand, until the source of her power flashed at me. Slowly, with an expression of utter malice in the eyes staring at me, she raised her other hand to cover the ring.

Her father had not turned to face her; he seemed

to have frozen. Now his face went from horror to
mindless rage. He whirled, his hand whipping across
his belly to his hilt. And for once in his life he moved
faster than she, and for once in his life he disci-
plined her.

The sword plunged into her naked belly, widen-
ing her navel into a long gash. As quickly he jerked it
out again, as a warrior does to release the gush of
blood.

Her eyes stared. She clapped her hands over the
wound. Blood streamed between her fingers. Her
mouth writhed soundlessly.

She disappeared—

—and reappeared.

And flickered, there and not-there—and then her
knees buckled and she fell forward on her face.

We stood there in silence. Complete silence; the par-
rot had hushed, and the wind had died with the
Guildmaster's daughter. He turned slowly from her.
The sword dripped.

"She . . . she's had me—and Brynda—in her thrall
for years. Since she was eight years old. Young . . .
and beautiful . . . and she's killed us both."

"Guildmaster," Stro Fentris said, "No. Come with
me, now. We'll get you out of the city. Itza . . . Azulthade . . ."

Shayhara backed from Fentris' outstretched hand.

"No. You'll make a good Guildmaster, Stro . . .
Brynda deserves a good Guildmaster, after me."
His eyes swerved to me. "It's dishonorable," he said.
"Unmanly . . . but I'm minded to kill you. As if all
this were your fault . . . because you dared defy both
her and me." He closed his eyes. "The Jadiriy of
Brynda," he said. To me.

Proby said, "But—Guildmaster! What will you
do?"

"Die," the Guildchief said, and he clasped both hands around the pommel of his sword and jerked its point to his sternum and lunged forward. He fell on the floor on his face; the sword that had transpierced his body tented his cloak. He jerked only twice.

We gave him a Guildchief's funeral.

The people insisted on the ritual enemy treatment of Solah's body.

All that was a long time ago. A long time.

I am Executive Secretary of a New Thing: the Interguild Council. Pretty much my invention. Not the concept, but the actuality and the formal post. I am liaison man among the Guilds of Brynda. At the beginning I set a (secret) goal, which is now about forty percent realized. I set out to break the power of the Warriors' Guild. Not by headlocking, meeting it with its weapons, but by slow dilution and erosion.

The rising power of the Artisans Guild helps.

We really should subdivide it; what does Pro Thoris' silversmithing have to do with my three alarm clock manufactures? (Rigging alarms to water clocks and hourglasses was easy. A sensitive weight takes care of it. The new alarm sundials, though, took some doing). Too, there are the safety-pin craftsmen—six of whom are my employees, since it was after all my invention. And the ready-made boot and sandal cobblers. And the two "plants" now making (water- or slook-powered) "electric fans."

Brynda is becoming an industrial state, phasing out the power of the warriors.

Dejah and I are of course cross fertile, and neither my figure nor hers is what it was. There are no bottle-babies on Aros.

Aros.

Phantasy world. The clue came from my father-in-law. Kro Kodres' cryptic message was to *me*.

A year after the deaths of the Jadiriyah and her father, when I was growing moneyed and powerful and gaining weight from both my Guilds-liaison job and my manufacturing enterprises, my wife presented me with the first of our three sons.

"I'll have to buy some gold," a beaming Pro Thoris said. "To make you a cup in honor of the golden cup of your mind, Big Head."

I stared at him.

Golden cup: Arone euphemism for the type of mind that sets things going. And bighead: *sorrfelinas*. I was suddenly aware that I had misunderstood the dying Kro Kodres. He hadn't said big *bones; zorveli nas*. He'd said *sorrfeli nas*: big*head*. "The golden cup is bighead." The mind that sets things going (on Aros) is bighead. But capitalize it: Bighead.

Even before I named Pope Borgia "Bighead," even before I knew Solah (Evelyn Shay, had she been here) was called "Bighead" (for a different reason), long before Pro called me Bighead. Solah: a sort of Arone simulacrum of Evelyn Shay. What she'd like to be, on such a world. Sexy, looking like her ideal woman, Liz Taylor. And powerful. A witch.

The mind that sets things going on Aros, Kro Kodres had been telling me—because he and his words were a part of the whole phantasy—is Bighead. And big-head is Evelyn Shay, *and* Pope Borgia, *and* Hank Ardor.

It hit me a few hours later, and the clouds of mystery began to dissipate as puzzle-pieces locked up. Sure, Aros is full of surprises and inconsistencies. It's a mental creation. *The creation of three minds.*

First, Evelyn's. She began it, postulating a Burroughs-type world. Realizing the place of a woman in a semibarbarian culture, she gave herself Power: she saw herself as a sorceress. (Childish as only an American woman can be; arrogant as befits a woman who is both a physics-Ph.D. candidate and—a ja-diriyah.)

Why "Aros?" Sounds like Eros, that's all. Why mirror-images? I'm not sure. Maybe whim. Maybe because that's what you *see*, and Evelyn was seeing herself here.

Kro Kodres was out there because I expected to find someone, and because I needed to know the language. Maybe Evelyn "put" him there, seeing herself as a noble Florence Nightingale with the wounded man —from whom she could learn the language. Maybe if she'd come here, he'd have been a prince. He wasn't for me because I just can't believe that sort of luck. (He had been, as it turned out, in the process of carrying off Solah. Which is why he had her ring.)

Telepathy: to facilitate learning the language. (Probably wouldn't work, but all those books say so, and Evelyn and I accepted it). It is still little used. Maybe because I don't think much about it.

The lighter gravity is standard Burroughs . . . but consider its effect on an Earthly woman's body. Up float breasts and innards; out goes the bosom and in goes the tummy. Evelyn Shay liked that concept, obviously.

Kro Kodres also provided a pleasantly, mysteriously cryptic phrase—which, rather than having to do with Arone affairs of state, was the solution to Aros itself. His message was to and for me.

He probably died, poor bastich, because I *thought* he would.

The reason for Evelyn/Solah's presence out there

on the desert: Maybe that was my idea. Damsel in distress, carried off by Kro Kodres. But it happened that said damsel was *Evelyn's* mental creation, not mine. So there I stood with egg on my face when she vanished. I suppose I arrived too late to prevent her Vardor rape because Evelyn and I both agreed that things were always too easy for hero *and* heroine on the barbar world. The girls are always grabbed, but never molested.

Part of Aros was created by Evelyn. Part of it I created, all unknowingly, and pretty much as I went along. And part, of course, is Pope Borgia's.

Expecting to find a jungle, he did. There aren't any snakes or predators or cockatoos because he didn't want any. And all the fruits were ripe, remember: for him. The men were Amazon-basin types because that's what *belonged* in a jungle, according to the gospel of Pope Borgia/Bighead. Still, he's a parrot, and he liked Dr. Blakey. So they wore lab smocks. And wouldn't it be nice if parrots ruled people, and told *them* what to say, and he was boss! So he was.

The jungle vanished behind us because he was concentrating on something else. It reappeared when he looked back, because he knew it was there. *(Cogito, ergo est.)* He found a caravan because I described one and hoped to find one, and he expected to. There was a road through the jungle because I assumed there would be.

There aren't any bees here because I hate honey. There *are* flies because, fool that I am, I *expected* them. Which is why Brynda looks like a city out of Flash Gordon, and a girl named Dejah Thoris (unimaginative me!) looks like Sophia Loren. And Frood/Freud has already lived, because I always thought

Man might have grown up if Freud and Darwin and Havelock Ellis had lived before Napoleon and Watts and Marco Polo. And the schlemiel who invented gunpowder.

Each item here was born, created, as we thought of it, expected it. And instantly it had always been, with history and a full explanation for its existence. (Why is Dejah's name Dejah? Obviously there could be no sensible explanation. So Pro remembered that her mother named her. And her mother's dead. And if I thought, from now till doomsday, her name to be Kate or Jodie or something, it would still be Dejah. There's no changing what's done. I've tried, with the flies, and with some mistakes I've made.)

Lalaikah. Well, I couldn't dope it out. I needed help. So: here was wise-grandmother-image Lalaikah. She said "No one should call one names but oneself, eh?" And that was the key to *her*. She was a creation of my subconscious. A message from me to me, because I *knew*, subconsciously, but my conscious mind needed help. So: Lalaikah. Strange, or perhaps not so strange: she died the day after I at last worked out the solution to the mystery of Aros.

There isn't and won't be a nation here with aircraft or bandaids—because I can't sincerely believe that there is.

How did I get here via a machine whose inventor called it a "temporal dissociator?" In the first place I don't know. But—part of the energy was Dr. Blakey's harnessing the electrical output of his own brain waves, as he himself said. And *my* brain waves, perhaps, and Evelyn's, and Pope Borgia's too. Also "within the bell," Blakey said, " 'reality' as we know it does not exist." He was right, strangely, without knowing it. Aros is—unreal.

Perhaps I can get this narrative back to Earth or to uh, Then/There (Here/Now, for you), by similar means. I am dictating it to the finest mental broadcaster(ess) I've met. IF some sort of electrical machinery is tuned in to me, back there, maybe the electrical output of her brain will imprint this oral narrative on a recorder, or something.

Aros is in my hands, now. Evelyn postulated; did a very rough pencil sketch. The inkwork and details are mine. And will be.

I'm in charge of details; I'm in charge of Aros, from here on out. I'm god, then.

Being god is lonely. I can't erase and start over (can god/God?). And I am a *worried* god.

Every day I meditate. Dejah and the kids humor me: Daddy's rich and getting richer, and awful mixed up in politics nowadays, and he has to get off by himself and think. I *can't* tell them that I am concentrating, with all my ability, on Aros' being real and permanent. Every day, very hard.

Because—I am the god *in* the machine. What about the deus *ex* machina, Evelyn? The original Aros, the concept, came from *her* mind.

What if Evelyn dies?

Every day in every way Aros is getting realer and realer. . . .

Evelyn Shay, wherever you are: LIVE!

endit